NASHVILLE – BOOK ONE – READY TO REACH

D1596330

NASHVILLE – BOOK ONE – READY TO REACH

INGLATH COOPER

Contents

Copyright

Published by Fence Free Entertainment, LLC
Copyright © Inglath Cooper, 2014
Cooper, Inglath

Publisher's Note

This is a work of fiction. Names, characters, places, and incidents are a product of the author's imagination. Locales and public names are sometimes used for atmospheric purposes. Any resemblance to actual people, living or dead, or to businesses, companies, events, institutions, or locales is completely coincidental.

Ever thought a dream might pass you by?

Nineteen-year old CeCe Mackenzie is determined to make her dreams come true. She heads for Nashville with not much more to her name than a guitar, a Walker Hound named Hank Junior and an old car she'd inherited from her grandma called Gertrude. But when Gertrude ends up on the side of I-40 in flames, Nashville has never seemed farther away. Help arrives in the form of two Georgia football players headed for the Nashville dream as well. When Holden Ashford and Thomas Franklin stop to offer CeCe and Hank Junior a ride, fate may just give a nod to serendipity and meant to be. Because while CeCe is chasing after her dream, she might find love as well.

CeCe

I've been praying since before I can ever actually remember learning how. Mama says I took to praying like baby ducks to their first dip in a pond, my "please" and "thank you" delivered in a voice so sweet that she didn't see how God would ever be able to say no to me.

Mama says my praying voice is my singing voice, and that anybody listening would know right off that the Father himself gave that voice to me. Two human beings, especially not her and one so flawed as the man who was supposedly my Daddy, would ever be able to create anything that reminiscent of Heaven.

I'm praying now. Hard as I ever have. "Dear Lord, please let this old rattletrap, I mean, faithful car Gertrude, last another hundred miles. Please don't let her break down before I get there. Please, dear Lord. Please."

A now familiar melody strings the plea together. I've been offering up the prayer for the past several hours at fifteen-minute intervals, and I'm hoping God's not tired of my interruptions. I've got no doubt He has way more important things on His plate today. I wonder now if I was a fool not to take the bus and leave the car behind altogether. It had been a sentimental decision, based on Granny's hope that her beloved Gertrude would help get me where I wanted to go in this life.

And leaving it behind would have been like leaving behind Hank Junior. I reach across the wide bench seat and rub his velvety-soft Walker Hound ear. Even above the rattle-wheeze-cough of the old car's engine, Hank Junior snores the baritone snore of his deepest sleep. He's wound up in a tight ball, his long legs tucked under him, his head curled back onto his shoulder. He reminds me of a duck in this position, and I can't for the life of me understand how it could be comfortable. I guess it must be, though, since with the exception of pee and water breaks, it's been his posture of choice since we left Virginia this morning.

Outside of Knoxville, I-40 begins to dip and rise, until the stretch of road is one long climb after the other. I cut into the right hand

1

lane, tractor-trailer trucks and an annoyed BMW whipping by me. Gertrude sounds like she may be gasping her last breath, and I actually feel sorry for her. The most Granny ever asked of her was a Saturday trip to Winn-Dixie and the post office and church on Sundays. I guess that was why she'd lasted so long.

Granny bought Gertrude, brand-spanking new, right off the lot, in 1960. She named her after an aunt of hers who lived to be a hundred and five. Granny thought there was no reason to expect anything less from her car if she changed the oil regularly and parked her in the woodshed next to her house to keep the elements from taking their toll on the blue-green exterior. It turned out Granny was right. It wasn't until she died last year and left Gertrude to me that the car started showing her age.

What with me driving all over the state of Virginia in the past year, one dive gig to another, weekend after weekend, I guess I've pretty much erased any benefits of Granny's pampering.

We top the steep grade at thirty-five. I let loose a sigh of relief along with a heartfelt prayer of thanks. The speedometer hits fifty-five, then sixty and seventy as we cruise down the long stretch of respite, and I see the highway open out nearly flat for as far ahead as I can see. Hank Junior is awake now, sitting up with his nose stuck out the lowered window on his side. He's pulling in the smells, dissecting them one by one, his eyes narrowed against the wind, his long black ears flapping behind him.

We're almost to Cookeville, and I'm feeling optimistic now about the last eighty miles or so into Nashville. I stick my arm out the window and let it fly with the same abandon as Hank Junior's ears, humming a melody I've been working on the past couple days.

A sudden roar in the front of the car is followed by an awful grinding sound. Gertrude jerks once, and then goes completely limp and silent. Hank Junior pulls his head in and looks at me with nearly comical canine alarm.

"Crap!" I yell. I hit the brake and wrestle the huge steering wheel to the side of the highway. My heart pounds like a bass drum, and I'm shaking when we finally roll to a stop. A burning smell hits my nose. I see black smoke start to seep from the cracks at the edge of the hood. It takes me a second or two to realize that Gertrude is on fire.

I grab Hank Junior's leash, snapping it on his collar before reaching over to shove open his door and scoot us both out. The flames are licking higher now, the smoke pitch black. "My guitar!" I scream. "Oh, no, my guitar!"

I grab the back door handle and yank hard. It's locked. Tugging Hank Junior behind me, I run around and try the other door. It opens, and I reach in for my guitar case and the notebook of lyrics sitting on top of it. Holding onto them both, I towboat Hank Junior around the car, intent on finding a place to hook his leash so I can get my suitcase out of the trunk.

Just then I hear another sputtering noise, like the sound of fuel igniting. I don't stop to think. I run as fast as I can away from the car, Hank Junior glued to my side, my guitar case and notebook clutched in my other hand.

I hear the car explode even as I'm still running flat out. I feel the heat on the backs of my arms. Hank Junior yelps, and we run faster. I trip and roll on the rough surface pavement, my guitar case skittering ahead of me, Hank Junior's leash getting tangled between my legs.

I lie there for a moment, staring up at the blue Tennessee sky, trying to decide if I'm okay. In the next instant, I realize the flouncy cotton skirt Mama made me as a going away present is strangling my waist, and Hank Junior's head is splayed across my belly, his leash wrapped tight around my left leg.

Brakes screech and tires squall near what sounds inches from my head. I rock forward, trying to get up, but Hank yips at the pinch of his collar.

"Are you all right?"

The voice is male and deep, Southern like mine with a little more drawl. I can't see his face, locked up with Hank Junior as I am. Footsteps, running, and then a pair of enormous cowboy boots comes into my vision.

"Shit-fire, girl! Is that your car?"

"Was my car," I say to the voice.

"Okay, then." He's standing over me now, a mountain of a guy wearing jeans, a t-shirt that blares Hit Me – I Can Take It and a Georgia Bulldogs cap. "Here, let me help you," he says.

He hunkers down beside me and starts to untangle Hank Junior's leash. Hank would usually do me the service of a bark if a stranger approached me, but not this time. He wags his tail in gratitude as the big guy unhooks the snap from his collar, tugs it free from under my leg and then re-hooks it.

Realizing my skirt is still snagged around my waist, my pink bikini underwear in full view, I sit up and yank it down, nothing remotely resembling dignity in my urgency.

"What's going on, man?"

I glance over my shoulder and see another guy walking toward us, this one not nearly so big, but sounding grouchy and looking sleep-deprived. He's also wearing cowboy boots and a Georgia Bulldogs cap, the bill pulled low over dark sunglasses. His brown hair is on the long side, curling out from under the hat.

He glances at the burning car, as if he's just now getting around to noticing it and utters, "Whoa."

Mountain Guy has me by the arm now and hauls me to my feet. "You okay?"

I swipe a hand across my skirt, dust poofing out. "I think so. Yes. Thank you."

Hank Junior looks at the second guy and mutters a low growl. I've never once doubted his judgment so I back up a step.

"Aw, he's all right," Mountain Guy says to Hank Junior, patting him on the head. "He always wakes up looking mean like that."

Grouchy Guy throws him a look. "What are we doing?"

"What does it look like we're doing?" Mountain Guy says. "Helping a damsel in distress."

"I'm not a damsel," I say, my feathers ruffling even as I realize I could hardly be in much more distress than I am currently in.

Gertrude is now fully engulfed in flames, from her pointed front end to her rounded trunk. Cars are keeping to the far left lane. Surprisingly, no one else has bothered to stop, although I can see people grabbing their cell phones as they pass, a couple to take pictures, others more likely dialing 911.

"So what exactly happened?" Mountain Guy asks me.

"I just heard this loud noise and then smoke started coming out of the hood."

"Good thing you got her pulled over fast," he says.

"I didn't know they let vehicles that old on the road," Grouchy Guy says.

"She belonged to my Granny," I fire back in instant outrage, as if everything that has just happened is all his fault.

Grouchy Guy starts to say something, presses his lips together, maybe thinking better of it.

"Don't pay him no mind," Mountain Guy advises. "You live near here?"

I laugh then, the sound popping up out of me under the sudden realization that with the exception of my dog, my guitar and my lyrics notebook, I now have no other earthly possessions to call my own. Even my purse has been incinerated inside Gertrude's melted interior.

The shrill whine of a fire engine echoes from down the Interstate, and a couple of seconds later it comes roaring into sight, lights flashing. It rolls to a heavy stop just behind Gertrude, brakes squealing. Men dressed in heavy tan uniforms grab hoses and run at the burning car.

The water gushes out with impressive force. The blazing fire is a joke against the onslaught, and in less than a minute, the flames slink into nothingness. The only thing left is the charred framework of Gertrude's once sleek exterior.

As soon as the water hoses cut off, I start to cry, as if some sort of transference has turned on the flow inside of me. I cry because I've ruined Granny's car, her most prized possession. I cry because I now have no money, no means of getting any closer to my dream than my own two feet will carry me. And I cry because everybody back home was exactly right. I was born with dreams way too big for somebody like me to ever make come true.

"Hey, now." Mountain Guy pats me on the shoulder the same way he had patted Hank Junior on the head a few minutes before. "Everything's gonna be all right."

One of the firemen walks up to us. "This y'all's car?"

Grouchy Guy points at me. "It was hers."

"Sorry for your loss, ma'am," the fireman says. "Guess you'll be needing to call a tow truck."

Even Mountain Guy can't help laughing at this, and maybe if you were removed from the situation, it would be pretty funny. Me? I'm anything but removed, and I'm suddenly thankful for Mama's faithful Triple A membership and the insurance she's paid up for me through the end of the year.

"You can tell them the car is just short of Mile Marker 320."

"Thank you," I say. "And thank you for putting out the–"

"No problem, ma'am," he says quickly, as if realizing I can't bring myself to finish.

I glance at Mountain Guy. "Do you have a cell I could borrow?"

"Sure thing." He pulls an iPhone from his shirt pocket and hands it to me.

"You mind if I get the number for Triple A?"

"'Course not."

Hank Junior's leash wrapped around my wrist, I walk a few steps away and tap 411. A bored-sounding operator gives me the 800 number and then connects me free of charge. The woman who takes my "case" doesn't sound the least bit surprised that my car has burned to smithereens or that I need a tow truck to come and get us both. I wonder if she gets calls like this every day.

In between her questions, I can hear Mountain Guy and Grouchy Guy in a low rumble of discussion that sounds like it has disagreement at its edges. I know they're talking about me, and while I want to swing around and scream at them both that I don't need their help, I know the last thing I can afford to do is look a gift horse in the mouth.

The lady from Triple A tells me that Ray's Towing from Cookeville will be coming out to get the car. She asks if I will also need a ride. I tell her both my dog and I will.

I return the phone to Mountain Guy.

"Get it all squared away?" he asks.

"I think so," I say, not even sure in this context what that could possibly mean.

"How long before they get here?"

"Hour."

"Well, you can't wait by yourself. It'll be dark by then," Mountain Guy says.

"I'll be fine," I say. "But thanks for stopping. And for letting me use your phone."

"Not a problem," he says, glancing over at Grouchy Guy who is still wearing his sunglasses and has his arms folded across his chest in a stance of non-compliance.

I pick up my guitar case and give Hank Junior a little tug before backing away from them. "Thanks again," I say and head for my charred car.

I'm halfway there when Mountain Guy calls out, "You going to Nashville?"

"What gave it away?" Grouchy Guy throws out, his voice heavy with sarcasm.

I pin him with a look, then turn my gaze to his friend. "Yeah. I am."

"Well, so are we," Mountain Guy says. "No point in you staying here when we're going to the same place, now is there?"

Relief, unwelcome though it is, floods through me. I am feeling kind of sick at the thought of waiting with the car while dark sets in. Maybe I've watched too many episodes of *Disappeared*. My imagination has already started heading off in directions I'd just as soon it didn't.

But then, on the other hand, I don't know squat about the two I'm getting ready to ride off with. They could be serial murderers thinking it was their lucky day that my car caught on fire, and they happened by.

Hank Junior seems to think they're all right though. He's no longer low-growling at Grouchy Guy. And besides, what choice do I really have? I have no money, no credit card, no clothes.

Panic starts to clutch at me, and all of a sudden, I hear my Granny's voice telling me, as she had so many times when I was growing up, that we take this life one moment, one day at a time. I'm not going to look any farther ahead than that because if I do, I think I might just dissolve into a puddle of failure right here on the side of I-40.

"Let's get this show on the road," Mountain Guy says, taking my guitar case from me and placing it in the bed of the pickup.

Grouchy Guy looks at me. "He riding in the back?"

"You mean Hank Junior?" I ask.

"That his name?"

"It is."

"Yeah, Hank Junior."

"Not unless I am," I answer.

Grouchy Guy looks at Mountain Guy. "That's fine with me."

Mountain Guy laughs. "Man, you got up on the wrong side of the truck." Then to me, "He ain't always this nasty. Y'all hop on in."

Without looking at Grouchy Guy, I scoot Hank Junior up onto the floorboard, and climb in behind him, sliding to the middle. He hops onto my lap and curls up in a ball, as if he knows he needs to be as inconspicuous as possible.

It's a full truck with the four of us. My shoulders are pressed up against both guys, and I try to make myself smaller by hunching over.

Mountain Guy throws the truck in gear, checks the side mirror and guns onto the highway. "Reckon we oughta know your name," he says.

"CeCe," I answer. "CeCe MacKenzie."

"CeCe MacKenzie," he sings back with a country twang. "Got a nice little rhyme to it."

"What's yours?" I ask, aware that I will now have to quit calling him Mountain Guy.

"Thomas Franklin."

"You don't look like a Thomas," I say.

"I get that a lot."

"I'm sorry," I start to apologize.

"Hey, no problem. My folks wanted the world to take me seriously, so they never gave in on the Tom, Tommy thing."

"Oh. Makes sense."

"Attitude over there is Holden Ashford."

"Hey," Holden says without looking at me. He's still wearing the dark glasses, and I wonder if his eyes are as unfriendly as his voice.

"Hey," I reply, matching my tone to his.

"Where you from, CeCe?" Thomas asks, shooting a glance my way.

"Virginia."

"Georgia," he says, waving a hand at himself and then Holden.

"Let me guess," Holden says. "You wanna be a singer?"

"I am a singer," I shoot back.

I can't be sure because of the glasses, but I'd swear he rolled his eyes. "What about the two of you? You headed to Nashville to be plumbers or something?"

Thomas laughs a deep laugh that fills up the truck. "Heck, no. I sing. He writes and plays guitar."

"That's why he takes himself so seriously." The words are out before I can think to stop them.

"Matter of fact, it is," Thomas says, another laugh rolling from his big chest.

"Up yours," Holden says without looking at either of us. I'm not sure if he's talking to Thomas or to me.

"What do you sing, CeCe?" Thomas asks.

"Country. What else is there?"

"Heck, yeah!" Thomas slaps the steering wheel. "Although with a dog named Hank Junior I reckon I could've assumed that."

At the sound of his name, Hank Junior raises his head, blinks at Thomas and then continues his snooze.

"What about you?" I ask. "Who're your favorites?"

"Chesney, Twitty, Haggard, Flatts. If it's got country on it, I sing it. Holden there says I have a sound of my own. I figure it's just what's managed to stick together from all my years of tryin' to sound as good as the greats."

The sun has dropped on the horizon, fading fast. The sky has a pinkish glow to it, and cars have started to flip on their headlights. A sign on the right says Cookeville – 5 miles.

Holden pulls a phone out of his pocket, taps the screen and says, "Starbucks off exit 288. I could use a coffee."

"I'll second that," Thomas agrees, and then looking at me, "We've got a gig tonight. Nine o'clock at the Bluebird."

"Seriously?" I say, not even bothering to hide my astonishment.

I've been reading about the Bluebird for years and the country music stars who played there before they made it big, Garth Brooks and Taylor Swift among them.

"Yeah," Thomas says. "You oughta come. I mean unless you got other plans."

Not unless you count finding a place to stay on credit. "I'd like that."

"Cool."

Holden makes a sound that clearly conveys his disapproval.

Irked, I say, "You ever take off those glasses? It's getting dark outside."

He looks directly at me then, without removing them. "They bothering you?"

"Honestly, yes. I like to judge a person by what I see in their eyes."

"Some reason you need to be judging me?"

"I don't know. Is there?"

He lowers the glasses and gives me a long cool look. His eyes are blue, ridiculously blue, and his lashes are thick. I lean away from him like I've been struck by a jolt of electricity.

"He's just lovesick," Thomas says. "He's harmless. Well, mostly. Depending on who you ask."

"Shut up," Holden says.

Thomas chuckles. "Oh, the tangled webs we weave in our wake."

"Good thing you're not the writer," Holden mutters.

"I had a little alliteration thing going on there," Thomas sings back.

I have to admit his voice is wonderful. Smooth and rolling like I imagine a really nice wine might taste.

"That's about all you had going," Holden says.

We're off the interstate now, turning left at a stoplight before swinging into the Starbucks on our right. Thomas pulls the truck into a parking spot. "Potty break, anyone?"

"Okay if Hank Junior waits here?" I ask.

"Sure, it is," Thomas says and then to Hank Junior, "you ever tried their mini donuts? No? How about I bring you one? Plain? Plain, it is."

I watch this exchange with a stupid grin on my face and wonder if

Thomas has any idea that the only thing anyone could ever do to make me like them instantly was be nice to my dog.

"I'll be right back, Hanky," I say, kissing the top of his head and sliding out of the truck on Thomas's side. I don't even dare look at Holden to get a read on his opinion of his friend's generos-ity. I'm pretty sure I know what it would be. And that's just gonna make me like him less.

Starbucks is crowded, tables and leather chairs occupied by every age range of person, their single common denominator the laptops propped up in front of them. The wonderful rich smell of coffee hits me in the nose, triggering a reminder that I haven't eaten anything since my last PBJ at eleven-thirty this morning. Right behind that comes the awareness that I have no money.

I head for the ladies' room, glad to find it empty. For once, the men's room has a line, and I don't relish the idea of standing in the hallway across from Grouchy Guy, exchanging glares.

A look in the bathroom mirror makes me wonder why those two bothered to give me a ride. My hair is a frizzy mess. What were wavy layers this morning have now conceded to chaotic turn screw curls that only need a BOIIING sound effect for maximum laugh value.

I pull an elastic band out of my skirt pocket and manage to tame the disaster into a ponytail. I splash water on my face, slurp some into my mouth and use my finger to pseudo brush my teeth. Looking up, I realize none of it has helped much but will just have to do for now.

I head to the front where Thomas and Holden are ordering. Line or not, they're fast.

"What do you want?" Thomas throws out. "I'll order yours."

"Oh, I'm good," I say, crossing my arms across my chest. "I'll just go let Hank Junior out."

Thomas points his remote at the parking lot and pushes a button. "That should unlock it. Sure you don't want anything?"

"I'm sure."

Outside, I open the truck door and hook up Hank Junior's leash. He bounds off the seat onto the asphalt, already looking for the nearest bush. I let him lead the way, across a grassy area to the spot of his choice. My stomach rumbles, and I tell myself this will be a good time to lose those five pounds I've been meaning to work on.

Hank Junior has just watered his third bush when I hear a shout, followed by the rev of an engine roaring off. Thomas and Holden are sprinting from Starbucks. At the truck door, Thomas looks around, spots me and waves frantically. "Come on!" he yells. "They just stole Holden's guitar!"

"They" are two guys on a motorcycle, now peeling out of the parking lot and hauling butt down the road. The guy on back has the guitar case wedged between them.

Hank Junior jumps in. I scramble up behind him. Thomas and Holden slam the doors, and Thomas burns rubber through the parking lot.

"You left the door standing wide open?" Holden shouts at me. He's not wearing his glasses now, and I have to say I wish I'd never asked him to take them off. His eyes are blazing with fury, and it's all directed at me.

"I was just a few yards away," I say. "I didn't think—"

"Something you're clearly not used to doing," he accuses between clenched teeth.

"Hey, now!" Thomas intervenes. "Y'all shut up! I'm planning on catching the sons of bitches."

And he's not kidding. Thomas drives like he was raised on Nascar, gunning around and in front of car after car.

"What's in the case?" I ask. "Diamonds?"

"Might as well be to Holden," Thomas says. "His lyric notebook."

My stomach drops another floor if that's possible. "Your only copy?"

"For all intents and purposes," he says.

By now, I'm feeling downright sick. I can feel Hank Junior's worry in the rigid way he's holding himself on my lap. I rub his head and say a prayer that we'll live to laugh about this. Every nerve in my body is screaming for Thomas to slow down, but a glance at Holden's face is all I need to keep my mouth shut.

"There they are!" I yell, spotting them up ahead just before they zip in front of a tractor-trailer loaded with logs.

"Crazy mothers," Thomas shouts, whipping around a Volvo whose driver gives us the finger.

I never liked thrill rides. I was always the one on church youth group trips to sit out the roller coaster or any other such thing designed to bring screams ripping up from a person's insides. I'm feeling like I might be sick at any moment, but I press my lips together and stay quiet.

"They just took a right," Holden barks. He unbuckles his seat belt and sticks his head out the window, yelling into the wind. I can't understand what he's saying, although I'm pretty sure it involves profanity.

"Why don't we just pull over and call 911?" I suggest.

Thomas ducks his head to see around a produce truck loaded with bushel baskets of tomatoes and cabbage. "They won't catch them before we do."

I have to admit we're gaining on them. I can now see the way the guy holding the guitar case keeps throwing looks of panic over his shoulder. He's making scooting motions, too, like he can force the motorcycle to go faster in doing so.

I drop my head against the seat and close my eyes, forcing myself not to look for a few seconds. That only makes the lack of control worse, so I bolt upright and hold onto Hank Junior tight as I can.

We're two car lengths behind them now, and the motorcycle driver has taken his craziness to another level. He zips past a mini-van, laying the bike so low that the end of the guitar case looks like it might touch the pavement. I hear and feel Holden yank in a breath.

Thomas cuts around the van and lays on the horn. We're right on the motorcycle's tail now and, in the headlights, I see that both the driver and his buddy are terrified. The front of the truck is all but touching the license plate of the motorcycle, and I don't dare think what would happen if they slammed on their brakes.

"Slow down!" I scream, unable to stand another second. At that same moment, the guy holding the guitar case sends it flying out to the right of the bike.

It skitters on the asphalt, slips under the rail and disappears from sight.

"Stop!" Holden yells.

Thomas hits the brakes, swings onto the shoulder and then slams the truck into reverse. Suddenly, we're backing up so fast my head is spinning.

"Right here!" Holden shouts and before Thomas has even fully stopped the truck, he's jumping out the door and running.

"There's a flashlight in the glove compartment," Thomas says, leaning over me.

I'm too stunned to move, and so I sit perfectly still, willing my reeling head to accept that we've stopped. Hank Junior barks his approval, and I rub his back in agreement.

Thomas hauls out, flicking on the flashlight and calling for Holden. Within seconds, he's disappeared from sight, too. I tell myself I need to get out and help look, but a full minute passes before I can force my knees to stop knocking long enough to slide off the truck seat. I hold onto Hank Junior's leash as if my life depends on it and teeter over to the spot where I'd seen them hop over the guardrail.

The drop off is steep, and vines cover the ground. I can't see much except in the swipes when cars pass and lend me their headlights. I catch a glimpse of the light way down the hill. I hear Thomas's voice followed by Holden's.

"Are y'all okay?" I call out.

"We got it!" Thomas yells.

I'm so relieved I literally wilt onto the rail, and send up a prayer of thanks. Hank Junior and I wait while they climb up. Holden appears first, looking as battered as his case. Thomas is right behind him. As soon as they reach the top, they both drop down on the ground, breathing heavily.

"Man," Thomas says. "What I wouldn't give for the chance to beat their tails!"

They gulp air for several seconds before Holden fumbles with the latches on the case and pops it open. Thomas points his flashlight at the interior, and my heart drops.

"Well, that's not good," Thomas says, his big Georgia voice dropping the words like boulders.

Holden picks up the guitar. It hangs limp and useless, broken in three places. He holds it the way a little boy would hold a baseball glove that got chewed up by the lawn mower. His expression is all but grief-stricken.

"I'm sorry," I say. "I'm so sorry."

"It wasn't your fault," Thomas consoles.

"Then whose fault is it?" Holden snaps, his blue gaze lasering me with accusation.

"Those two butt-wipes who stole it," Thomas says tightly.

"None of this would have happened if you hadn't insisted on stopping to help her!"

"Man, what's wrong with you? Her car was on fire. Chivalry ain't that dead."

Holden hesitates, clearly wrestling with a different opinion. "We didn't have to give her a ride to Nashville."

"No, we didn't," Thomas agrees. "But that ain't who we are."

I stand and dust off my skirt. I walk to the truck, Hank Junior trailing behind me. I climb up on the back tire, reach for my guitar and return to where the two of them are still sitting. I pull out my own lyric notebook and the flash drive that contains the only two song demos I've been able to afford to have made. I stick that in my pocket, close the case and hand it to Holden.

"You take mine," I say. "I know it won't replace yours, but maybe it'll work temporarily. Y'all have been real nice to me. I'm not gonna ask any more of you. Thanks a lot for everything."

And with that, Hank Junior and I start walking.

Holden

I don't want to stop her.

I mean, what the hell? You don't need to be a friggin' genius to see the girl's nothing but trouble.

"You just gonna let her walk off into the night?" Thomas asks, looking at me like I just destroyed every illusion he ever had about me.

"If she wants to go, who are we to stop her?"

"You know dang well she thinks, knows, you don't want her riding with us."

"Do we really need another card stacked against us? She's a walking disaster!"

Thomas throws a glance up the highway. "Yeah, right now she is."

"See. You're already trying to figure out how to fix things for her. Every time you find somebody that needs fixing, we come out on the losing end of the deal."

"If you're talkin' about Sarah, that's your doin', man. All I ever agreed to do with her was sing. You're the one who got involved with her. Nobody made you do that but you."

I'd like to tell him to piss off, as a matter of fact. Except that he's right.

I get to my feet, slap the dirt from my jeans and yank up both cases, one containing my broken Martin, the other holding the piece of crap CeCe MacKenzie probably bought at Wal-Mart.

"You keeping the guitar?" Thomas calls from behind me.

"I'll toss it out the window when we pass her," I say.

"Oh, that's mature."

I put both the guitars in the back, giving lie to what I just said. I climb in the truck and slam the door. Thomas floors it, merging into the oncoming traffic.

Thomas hunches over the steering wheel, looking for her. I'm starting to wonder if, hope, she's hitched another ride when I spot her up ahead, her skirt flouncing left to right as she walks, that ridiculous floppy-eared hound trotting along beside her.

"Well?" Thomas throws out.

"Pull the hell over," I say.

He looks at me and grins but knows better than to say anything. Wheeling the truck to a stop in front of her, Thomas gets out and walks around back. I force myself not to look in the side mirror. I crank the radio, lean against the seat and close my eyes.

A couple of minutes pass before the two of them walk to the driver's side and climb in.

Hank Junior licks my face and I jerk forward, glaring at him. "You have to write her an invitation?" I ask. "We're supposed to be in Nashville in an hour and a half."

"Ain't no problem," Thomas says. "We'll be there with warm-up time to spare."

Thomas grabs his Starbucks bag from the dash where he'd flung it earlier. He pulls out a plain mini-donut and offers it to Hank Junior. "Believe I promised you that."

The dog takes it as if he's royalty sitting down to tea. He chews it delicately and licks his lips. "Good, ain't it?" Thomas says, pleased. "Got you one, too, CeCe."

"That's okay," she says.

"Go on, now. Hank Junior and I can't eat alone."

She takes the donut from him and bites into it with a sigh of pure pleasure. "Um, that's good. Thank you."

"You're welcome."

CeCe sits straight as an arrow, Hank Junior curled on top of her again. She's yet to look at me, and I can imagine her pride has taken a few more pokes in agreeing to get back in here with us.

"I'm real sorry about your guitar," she says in a low voice. "I mean it about you taking mine. My uncle used to play with a group called The Rounders. He gave it to me before he died."

"The Rounders?" I say, recognizing the name. "They wrote 'Wish It Was True' and 'Long Time Comin'?"

"Yeah, those were their biggest songs," she says, still not looking at me.

"That's some good music," Thomas says. "I've had both those tunes in my sets."

"Me, too," CeCe says.

I stay quiet for a moment. "Which one was your uncle?"

"Dobie. Dobie Crawford."

"Good writer," I say, not sure why it's so hard for me to release the compliment since I really do mean it. "I didn't realize he'd died."

"Two years ago," she says.

"What happened to him?" Thomas asks.

"Liver failure."

"That's a shame," he says.

"Yeah," I add. "It is. I'm sorry."

"Thanks," she says, looking at me now with surprise in her voice. "He was a good man. Aside from the drinking, I mean."

"He teach you how to play?" Thomas asks.

"He did," she says. "I was five when he started giving me lessons."

"You any good?" I ask, unable to stop myself.

She shrugs. "He thought I was."

We're looking at each other now, and all of a sudden it's like I'm seeing her for the first time. I realize how unfair I've been to her, that I deliberately set out not to see her as anything more than a noose around our necks.

"What do you think?"

"I think I'm pretty good. Not nearly as good as he was."

"Not many people have a teacher with that kind of talent."

"I was lucky," she says. "Who taught you?"

"I mostly taught myself," I say.

"Don't let him fool you," Thomas says. "He's got the gift. Plays like God Himself is directing his fingers."

"Wow." She looks at me full on, as if she's letting herself take me in for the first time, too, without the conclusions she's already made about me getting in the way. I'm uncomfortable under her gaze, and I don't know that I can say why. An hour ago, I didn't care what she thought of me.

"Thomas just likes the fact that he doesn't have to pay me to play for him," I say, throwing off the compliment.

"That's a plus for sure," Thomas says, and then to CeCe, "but I still ain't overselling him."

"I'd like to hear you play," she says, glancing at me again.

"Good," Thomas says. "'Cause he's gonna have to take you up on that guitar of yours. We're onstage in less than an hour."

"Okay then if I come watch?" she asks in a cautious voice.

"Sure, it is," Thomas says.

CeCe looks at me, expecting me to disagree, I would guess. But I don't. "I don't want your guitar. To keep, I mean. I'll borrow it just for tonight."

"You can keep it," she says. "I owe you."

"I don't want your guitar."

"Okay."

♪

WE DRIVE THE REST of the way into Nashville without saying too much of anything. Thomas has gone quiet in the way he always does before a show, playing through lyrics in his head, gathering up whatever emotional steam he needs to get up in front of an audience and sing.

We've been together long enough that we respect each other's process, and when it comes time to leave each other alone, we do.

I air guitar some chord patterns, walk through a new tune we're doing at the end of the set tonight, wonder if I could improve the chorus lyric.

CeCe's head drops against my shoulder, and it's only then I realize she's asleep. Hank Junior has been snoring the past ten miles. I look down at CeCe and will myself not to move. I don't know if it's because she's clearly dead tired or because her hair is so soft on my arm. I can smell the shampoo she must have used that morning. It smells clean and fresh, like springtime and honeysuckle.

I feel Thomas look at me, but I refuse to look at him. I know what he's thinking. That's when I move closer to the door, and CeCe comes awake with a start.

"Oh," she says, groggy, "I'm sorry. I didn't realize I dozed off."

"It's okay," I say, wondering if I could be more of an ass.

CeCe sits upright as a poker the rest of the way into the city. Hank Junior goes on snoring, and she rubs his ears, first one, then the other.

Thomas drives straight to the Bluebird. We've been coming down every few weeks for the past year or so, working odd jobs back home, saving money, gathering proof each time we come that we need to give this a real shot. This time, we're staying.

The strip mall that includes the Bluebird Café among its tenants isn't much to look at from the outside.

The lot is full so we squeeze into a grassy area not too far from the main entrance. The place is small, the sign out front nothing that will knock your socks off.

"It's not exactly what I imagined." CeCe studies the front door. "I thought it would be bigger."

"We thought the same thing first time here," Thomas agrees.

The truth is we'd felt downright disappointed. Both of us had heard about the place for years, how many dreams had come to fruition behind those doors. The physical appearance had been something of a letdown. It's not until you're inside and witness what goes on there that you get the fact that the appearance doesn't much matter.

"Hank Junior can wait here," Thomas says. "That okay?"

"Yeah," CeCe says. "Let me take him potty first."

Hank Junior follows her out of the truck as if that's exactly what he had on his to do list. They head for a grassy spot several yards away where Hank Junior makes use of a light pole.

Thomas reaches for CeCe's guitar case. "Maybe you oughta tune her up."

"Yeah," I say, taking the case and setting it at my feet. I feel weird about it even though I know CeCe wants me to use it. I pull out the guitar, pleasantly surprised by the heft of it. It's a Martin, like mine, and this too, catches me off guard. I guess I should have known if it belonged to Dobie Crawford, it was gonna be more than decent.

I sit on the curb, strum a few chords, and find there's not much to improve on. CeCe knows how to tune a guitar.

She's back then, Hank Junior panting like he's thirsty. "Either of you have a bottle of water you could share with Hank?"

I stand up, reach under the truck seat and pull out one I'd opened earlier.

"Thanks," she says, without looking me in the eye. She takes the cap off, squats in front of the dog and cups her hand, letting him drink from it. She refills her palm until he loses interest, and then she helps him up in the truck.

Thomas hits the remote. "Let's get on in there."

"Ah, would it be all right if I borrow some money for the cover charge? I. . .my wallet was in the car."

"You have no money?" I ask before I think to soften or censor the question.

She shakes her head, glancing down at her sandals. She looks up then, pride flashing in her eyes. "I'll pay you back."

"No need to be worrying about that," Thomas intervenes. "We'll spot you what you need. You don't have to pay here anyway. You're with the band."

I attempt to level Thomas with a look, but our friendship is way past the point of him giving in to me on anything he doesn't want to. "You're using her guitar, aren't you?" he tosses at me in case I need an explanation.

I start to argue that I wouldn't need her guitar if she hadn't left the truck door open. That seems pointless right now, so I march on ahead of them without bothering to reply.

There's a crowd, college kids, couples, older folks, pretty much the gamut. I step around the line, murmuring, "Excuse me, sorry." I duck through the door, trying not to bump anyone with the guitar case, Thomas and CeCe behind me.

A dark-haired girl is working the front door. She's wearing a short blue dress, scooped low, and cowboy boots that make her legs seem a mile long. She directs a high beam smile at me. "You in the round?"

"We are," I say, waving a hand at Thomas and CeCe.

"What about her?" She looks at CeCe and forces a smile the way girls do when they sense competition.

"She's with us," Thomas says.

"Are you playing?" the girl asks, meeting CeCe's gaze with a note of authority.

"I, no–" CeCe begins.

"Then you'll need to pay the cover charge," she says.

Thomas starts to pull out his wallet when she adds, "And go to the back of the line. All these other people were here before you."

CeCe's eyes go wide, and suddenly bright like she's going to bust out crying at any second. I guess it has been that kind of day for her.

I lean in on the stand, close to the girl's face and say, "Can you cut her a break just for tonight? I'm using her guitar because mine got stolen by two guys on a motorcycle."

"Hey!" Someone yells from the end of the line. "We standin' here all night or getting inside to hear some music?"

"All right, all right," the girl says, not taking her eyes off mine while she writes something on a card and hands it to me. "I'm Ashley. Call me later. I'd like to hear the rest of your story."

I slip it in my shirt pocket and start making my way through the tables to the center of the floor where other writers and singers are already set up.

"So that's why you bring him along," I hear CeCe say to Thomas.

"Gotta admit he comes in handy," Thomas shoots back with a laugh.

Thomas and I take the two chairs remaining in the circle. We've met everyone else in the round on other trips to Nashville. Darryl Taylor to my left who I just heard is on the cusp of a record deal. He writes his own stuff, and he's good. Really good. Shauna Owens sits next to Thomas. She's been a semi-finalist on Idol, and I hear the only thing keeping her from the big leagues is her stage fright. Sometimes she keeps it under wraps, and sometimes she doesn't.

Across from us is a fifteen-year old who's been coming to town with her mom for the past two years, learning the ropes, writing at first with anyone she could find. Last time we were in town, writers were starting to seek her out, which means someone up the ladder is taking notice of her.

Within ten minutes, the place is totally packed. People are turned away at the door. I look around and spot CeCe leaning against a corner wall by the bar. She looks a little lost standing there by herself, and I feel a pang of compassion for her. I instantly blink it away, reminding myself that Thomas and I both will do well if we manage to navigate the waters of this town without either one of us drowning. We threw her a life raft today. That oughta be enough. I'm not about to take on swimming her to shore.

Mike Hanson is top dog in the round tonight. He's got a publishing deal with one of the major houses in town and just recently got his first cut with a cool new band. Thomas and I met him when we started coming to town and playing at the Listening Room. He'd already been at it for a couple of years then, and starting to get some interest. I knew the first time I heard him that he had the talent to make it, but the way things work here, affirmation doesn't come until you get a publishing deal. The next rung up is a cut.

Mike blows on the microphone, taps it once and makes it squawk. "Howdy, everybody. Welcome to the Bluebird Café. I'd like to thank y'all for coming out. I'm Mike Hanson. We got some fine music for you tonight."

The crowd claps with enough enthusiasm that it's clear they believe him. I'm hoping we live up to it.

Mike introduces each of us, calls me and Thomas a duo, singer-writer team, and I start to get a rush of nerves the way I always do just before we perform.

"Y'all don't forget your waiters and waitresses tonight," Mike reminds the crowd. People clap and whistle. Mike strums a few chords. "I hope y'all will be hearing this on the radio real soon." He sets right in to the song then, and the applause grows louder. It's clear word has gotten out about his recent success.

This is one thing I've come to love about Nashville. People here take pleasure in the accomplishment of others. Sure, everyone wants to make it, or they wouldn't have come in the first place. It's more than that though, a camaraderie of a sort I haven't known anywhere else.

It's almost like running some kind of marathon together, and instead of begrudging the fact that they've crossed the finish line before you, you're somewhere behind them, throwing a fist in the air and cheering them on.

At least, the people who have been at it a while do. Don't get me wrong. The competition is fierce. Thomas and I were no different from any other newbie to the scene. We drove into town almost a year ago, thinking we'd be on the radio in no time. We'd gotten enough validation from our fans back home on the University of Georgia scene that we'd started to accept their loyalty as all we needed to verify what would happen once Nashville discovered us.

What we hadn't counted on was all the other talent riding into town on the same wave of determination and hope. And how damn good they would be.

Mike's song is enough to make me green with envy if I let myself buy into that. The lyrics are raw with truth, but polished like a diamond that's been buffed with a soft cloth. The music has an element of something different enough to make it sound fresh, make it stand out.

I don't think I'm far enough along to know exactly what it is that sets it apart from what the rest of us will play tonight. I just know there is something, and more than anything in the world, I want my stuff to be that good. A year of coming here has shown me that it's not, yet, and in some weird and kind of awful way, I guess you could call that growth.

When Mike repeats the last tag of his song, the crowd throws out a storm of applause. He's shy, and makes a pretense of brushing something off the front of his guitar, then leans into the microphone again. "Thank y'all. Thank you so much."

When the applause falls back, the fifteen-year old sitting next to Mike starts her song, and while the lyrics don't have the power of Mike's, her voice is soft and sweet, the tone unique enough that it's easy to see she's got something special. People lean forward in their chairs, caught up on the wings of it, the emotion she lets spill through each word, captivating in and of itself.

Two more writers are up before Thomas and me. They're both good, better than good, and I'm feeling the pressure of comparison. Thomas takes the microphone and glances at me the way he does when he's ready. I tip into the intro, hitting the strings so lightly, that a hush falls over the room, and I can feel them start to listen.

I wrote this song for Thomas. His little sister died of cancer when he was twelve, and I remember how I felt when he told me about it, what it was like to go to the hospital to see her, watch her be strong for him, even though she was younger than he was, even as the pain became unbearable. I tried to write the lyric as if I'd been standing in that room, as if I had been Thomas, a big brother who's got to know what it will be like where she's going, that he will see her again one day.

I wrote it from a father's point of view, somehow knowing I needed to give Thomas that distance. That he would never get through the song singing it as the brother.

It's called Up There, and he sings it now like his own truth. I guess that's why what the two of us have works.

I can see the faces of the people directly in front of us, the glimmer of tears in their eyes. Maybe this is what I love most about writing, that moment when you realize you've hit a universal, something everyone can feel.

I'm drawn to look up then and find CeCe's gaze on me. I see on her face what I have felt on my own so many times. That yearning to express something that reaches people the way this song is doing. I glimpse enough of myself in her then that I wonder why I've been so hard on her, why I'd assumed she would want to stay in the shallow end of this pool. The look in her eyes tells me something completely different. She's headed for the deep end, wants it with all her soul. And I don't doubt for a second that she won't give up until she's there, swimming on her own.

A long moment of silence follows Thomas's last note. One person starts to clap. More follow until the room is alive with it. Thomas never finishes this song without tears in his eyes, and tonight is no exception.

Mike is next again, and as good as his song is, I think I can honestly say, its effect on the audience doesn't top ours.

The round goes on for four more songs each. Thomas and I do a fast one, a slow one and then another fast one. When it's our turn to do our last song, he looks over at me before glancing out to where CeCe is still standing against the wall. I don't think she's moved all night, and I remember the first time I came here, how I'd just sat listening, not moving once until the end of the show.

"If y'all don't mind, I'm gonna bring a new face in for this one. CeCe, come on up, girl."

She stands frozen, her expression a confused mixture of euphoria and disbelief, as if she can't decide whether to run or sink onto the floor. Thomas isn't about to let her do either one. I'm suddenly so mad at him, I can't see straight. What the heck is he doing? She's not ready for this!

But the crowd has turned their attention to her, and someone starts to clap, urging her on. There's a whistle, then another, more clapping until the force of it peels her off the wall and propels her to the circle of chairs.

Her eyes are wide as dinner plates, and I'm starting to wonder if she's ever actually been on stage before.

Thomas pats one enormous thigh and indicates for her to sit, placing the microphone stand close in to them both.

"This here's CeCe MacKenzie. CeCe's new in town, and she's had a bit of a rough day. We'll make this her Nashville welcome. Y'all might've heard of her uncle, Dobie Crawford with the Rounders."

The applause erupts into a roar then. I'm hoping for CeCe's sake and for ours that she lives up to expectation.

"Dobie wrote a song called 'Wish It Were True'," Thomas continues. "Let's do that one for them," he says to both me and CeCe.

It's been a while since we've done this one. Luckily, I know it like I wrote it myself.

Thomas starts in on the first verse, and by the third line, I'm wondering if CeCe is going to join in. She closes her eyes and follows him into the chorus, her voice floating up in perfect harmony against Thomas's.

I'm shocked by the blend. The sound is like chocolate and peanut butter. French coffee and half and half.

They've never sung together, and they sound like they've been doing so their whole lives. They each know the song the way you can only know one when its meaning reflects something of your own life.

By the second verse, it's clear that CeCe's forgotten she's sitting on the knee of a guy she just met today. Forgotten she's singing to a crowd at the Bluebird. I don't know where she is, but it's a place that lets her sing from the heart, from the soul.

I don't hear training in her voice. It's not perfected in that way. What I hear is a girl who's been singing all her life. A girl who sings because it's what she loves more than anything.

They hit the second chorus full throttle, and they're smiling at each other, all out joy lighting their faces. The crowd is with them, sitting up on the edge of their chairs. I can see their realization that they are witnessing something they'll talk about one day. "I saw them when they were just starting out. The very first time they ever sang together."

And I have to admit, it's like that. Some kind of magic that makes me wonder if everything that happened today had been the lead in to this. If we were supposed to meet her. Both for her sake and for ours.

They trail off, note for note, and the applause that follows is the loudest of the night. CeCe has tears in her eyes when she throws her arms around Thomas's neck and hugs him so hard, he nearly sends the chair over backwards. People laugh and clap harder.

I watch for a moment longer, and then unable to help myself, I clap, too.

CeCe

I feel like I'm in the middle of a dream. The good part where you're aware of hoping you don't wake up. That it will go on and on forever.

I'm hugging Thomas as tight as I can because I don't trust myself to thank him with words. If I do, I'll break down and sob right here in front of all these people.

He hugs me hard and stands, his arm still around my waist. I dangle in mid-air for a moment, then slide down his big thigh until my feet hit the floor. He forces me to face the crowd, and I'm blown away by the admiration and appreciation on their faces.

I feel Holden's gaze on me and make myself look at him. I guess I'm expecting him to be mad at me for horning in on their show, but that's not what I see in his eyes. What's there is the same admiration the audience has offered up, and maybe that surprises me most of all.

Mike thanks everyone again for coming, and people start to stand up and push their seats back. Several weave their way up to the circle of chairs and begin talking with the performers. A couple of teenagers ask Mike for his autograph. Next, they laser in on Thomas and Holden, giggling and looking as if they might lose their nerve at any moment.

One of the girls has red hair that hangs to her waist. Her eyes are a vivid green, and she looks at Thomas with starstruck longing. "Would you sign this for me?" she asks, handing him a Bluebird napkin.

"Why, sure, I will." Thomas raises an eyebrow at Holden who shakes his head.

"You're gonna be famous one day, Thomas," the girl says. "I just know it."

Thomas grins. "If that means I get to sing for a living, I'd be all right with that."

The redhead's friend sticks out a napkin of her own. "We'll buy anything you release."

"You don't work for a record company, do you?" Holden throws out.

Both girls giggle. "We're fifteen."

"Shoot," Thomas says. "Just our luck."

They laugh again, and then the redhead looks at me, her voice suddenly shy. "Your singing's so pretty."

Something in the sincerity of the compliment touches me, makes instant tears well in my eyes. It's stupid, I know, but after the way this day has gone, it's nice to hear that I'm not totally crazy to think I might have a place here. "Thank you," I say. "Thank you so much."

"You're welcome," she says, ducking her head again.

The two girls bounce off, clutching their napkins to their chests like they'd just found winning lottery tickets.

A man walks up and introduces himself. "I'm Clay Morrison. Y'all sounded real good tonight."

He has dark hair that's started to pepper a bit at the sides. He's dressed in jeans and a white shirt under a black jacket. His shoes are black, too, and they look expensive. Narrow frame glasses tone down his good looks and suggest he's smart.

I step out of the circle so his focus is on Thomas and Holden.

"Thank you," Thomas says. "Appreciate that."

"Saw you two here a few months ago. Have to say I like your new addition. The three of you sound pretty great together."

He swings a look at me then, and I want to sink into the floor. The last thing I want to do is barge in on their action. And it feels like that's what I'm doing. "Excuse me," I say and head for the ladies' room.

I lock myself inside, leaning against the door and pulling in a deep, shaky breath. I can still feel Holden's gaze on me, resentful, accusing.

I wash my face and dry it with a scratchy brown paper towel, taking my time with the process until I think Thomas and Holden might be ready to leave.

When I come out again, they're both waiting by the front door.

"You fall in?" Holden asks, looking me up and down.

I roll my eyes at him, pushing out into the cool of the Nashville evening.

We walk to the truck in an awkward silence, like neither of us knows what to say about what happened in there tonight.

Thomas hits the remote, and I open the door. Hank Junior leaps out and heads for the closest bush. I grab his leash and follow him.

When we return, it's clear Thomas and Holden have been talking. There's electricity in the air, the kind that sparks from disagreement.

Neither one looks at me, and I'm thinking it's time I go my own way. "Hey, thanks for everything, y'all. The help, the ride, the song. I expect to see your names in big places."

Hank Junior wants to jump in, but I stop him. "Come on, boy," I say, then turn around and start walking.

I have no earthly idea where I'm going. I just know I need to get away from those two before I bawl like a three-year old. I'm walking so fast that Hank Junior has to trot to keep up with me. He keeps looking back at the truck and then up at me as if he's wondering what in the world I'm doing. I wouldn't know how to begin to answer him. I don't have a thing to my name except for him. Should I find a pay phone, call Mama right now and ask her to buy me a bus ticket home? Could I even take Hank Junior with me on a bus?

I cross the main road in front of the Bluebird. There's a parking garage there. Maybe we can camp out for the night and see how things look in the morning, although short of me finding a winning lottery ticket in my pocket, I don't know how it could look any better.

The garage is nearly empty, a few cars parked along the other side that opens through to a Whole Foods. My stomach does a low rumble, and I know Hank Junior has to be hungry as well.

I head for a corner and lean against the wall, sliding down onto the cold concrete. Hank Junior looks at me as if he isn't sure what he's supposed to do. I pat the spot next to me, and loyal friend that he is, he curls up with me, his head on my knee.

That's when the tears start up for real. They gush from me like a geyser, and I just let them pour out, helpless to stop them even if I wanted to.

Hank Junior anxiously licks them from my cheek, and I rub his side, his sweetness making me drop my head to my knees and cry harder.

I guess it's my own sobbing that keeps me from hearing the truck until it stops right in front of us.

"This your plan?"

I jerk my head up to see Holden looking down at me with

resignation on his face, like he's finally given in to the idea that they are stuck with me.

"For this minute, it is," I shoot back.

"Sleeping in a parking garage?"

"Does it look like I'm sleeping?"

"It looks like you're crying."

"Since when is that illegal?"

"Get in the truck, CeCe."

"No," I say. "I'll be fine."

"Oh, you've been doing a great job of proving that," he throws out.

"I didn't ask you to rescue me!"

"And I sure as heck didn't volunteer for the job," he says, opening the door and swinging out.

I pop to my feet, the concrete scratching at my back through my thin cotton shirt.

"Are you coming with us or not?"

"I don't need your charity, Holden!"

He leans in like a football player aiming a tackle and hefts me over his shoulder. I start kicking and wriggling, but he tightens his hold like I'm a sack of grain. Hank Junior stands there looking up at us, wagging his tail.

I'd like to think Holden is being chivalrous or some such thing. The truth is he's mad and altogether tired of me messing up his plans.

"When you two get finished with the foreplay, hop on in, and we'll go get some sleep," Thomas tosses out the open door.

Holden walks to the truck with me still slung over his shoulder. "Get in, boy," he says to Hank Junior who hops in like he's in the middle of a raging ocean, and Holden just threw him a buoy.

Holden tilts forward and drops me in beside Hank Junior. Fury has me sputtering some not so ladylike protests. My skirt is up around my waist for the second time today, and I kick and struggle to sit up and pull it down.

Thomas laughs and shakes his head. "You two are right entertaining."

Clearly, neither of us finds his assessment amusing.

Holden climbs in and slams the door. "Can we go now?"

Thomas peels out of the parking garage and turns right, gunning it. "I'm starving," he says. "Next stop, food."

He swings into a McDonald's, pulling up at the drive-through lane. At the window, he places his order, two big Macs, two fries, a large Coke, then looks at me and says, "What do you want?"

"I'm fine, thanks," I say.

Holden rolls his eyes. "Would you quit pretending like you have any other choice but to accept our help right now?"

"Seriously, CeCe," Thomas says.

The pride trying to raise a flag inside me wilts. "Unsweetened iced tea. Mushroom and Swiss burger, please. With no meat."

"No meat?" Thomas repeats, as if I'd just made the request in Mandarin.

"You mean like a cheese sandwich?" Holden says.

"Just no meat," I answer.

Both guys look at each other and shake their heads. Thomas calls out Holden's order, which is a duplicate of his own, adding, "We'll take two plain burgers and a water, too."

He pats Hank Junior on the head, and then to me, "I'm assuming our buddy here is not a vegetarian?"

"No," I say. "And thank you."

"You're entirely welcome," Thomas says, pulling forward.

We get the food and tear into the bags as if none of us has eaten in days. I open up Hank Junior's, force him to wait a few moments until it cools, then take pity on his drooling and let him have it.

Thomas drives while he eats, and it isn't until my stomach is full that I think to ask, "Where are we going?"

"We've got an apartment over by Vanderbilt," Holden says. "Don't have any furniture yet, but at least we have a floor to sleep on."

I don't even bother to object. A place to sleep right now sounds so good I melt at the thought of it, fatigue pulling at every bone, every muscle.

Thomas parks the truck on the street, and they grab their suitcases from the back. Holden hands me my guitar case, before reaching for his own. I follow them up the walk, stopping in a grassy spot to let

Hank Junior do his business. They wait for us at the main door, before we climb a set of stairs to the third floor.

Holden pulls out a key and opens up the apartment, flicking on a light. The living room and kitchen aren't huge, but the place is neat and clean, the walls a newly painted beige.

"We've got two bedrooms. Holden and I will bunk up," Thomas says. "You and Hank Junior take the other one."

"I'll be happy to sleep out here," I say.

"We're good." Holden's words are short and abrupt. He heads down the hallway and disappears inside one of the rooms.

I look at Thomas and say, "I don't know how to thank you."

"You don't need to," Thomas says. "Go get some sleep."

I find the bedroom, wave Hank Junior inside and close the door. There's a bathroom that connects. I turn on the faucet and splash my face with water, leaning in to drink some, then rinse and spit since I don't have a toothbrush. I've brought in Hank Junior's McDonald's cup. I fill it with water and set it inside the bedroom, up against a wall. He saunters over and takes a couple laps, then flops down beside it, lowers his head on his paws and closes his eyes.

I make use of the toilet and flip off the light, lying down beside him on the floor and using his soft side as a pillow.

There are no curtains in the room, and a streetlight throws a beam across the middle of the floor. I try to turn off my brain, make all the what-if's and how-will-I's stop their relentless pecking, at least until morning, when I can address them with something resembling clear thinking.

I attempt sleep for an hour or more, but it's no use. My brain just won't turn off. I get up and leave the room, closing the door softly behind me to keep from waking up Hank Junior.

I walk through the living room and open the sliding glass door that leads onto a small deck. Holden is leaning on the railing, staring at the dark street below.

"Oh, I'm sorry," I say. "I didn't realize you were out here."

He looks over his shoulder at me, and I can see his hair is damp from a shower. "You can't sleep either?" he asks, his voice even now, without the threads of irritation and aggravation I'd heard in it earlier.

"No. Even though I'm pooped."

"I'm not a big sleeper," he says. "Plus Thomas snores."

"You can take the room I'm in," I say. "Really."

He shakes his head. "We were roommates in college. If I'm in sleep mode, I don't even hear him."

I step closer to the railing, folding my arms across my chest. "How long have you two known each other?"

"We met freshman year."

"Football?"

"Yeah."

"When did you start the music thing?"

"Both of us for as long as we can remember. Together, pretty much right after we met."

I nod and say, "Y'all are quite a match."

"Thanks. We kinda get each other."

"Not the easiest thing to come by."

"This what you've always wanted to do?"

"Yeah. I loved watching Uncle Dobie with his band. He told me one time that the way to know if music was going to be your life was to decide whether or not you were willing to give everything else up for it. He never got married or had a family."

"You think it's gotta be like that?" he asks, looking at me.

"I think dreams can have a high price tag or everyone would be going after them."

"Guess that's true."

"What did you leave behind to come here?" I ask.

"Why do you think I left something behind?"

"What's her name?"

He throws a glance at the street and then turns to me. "Sarah."

"Ah. Why didn't she come with you?"

"She likes predictability. Security. About the only thing I can predict is that I will write another song. Even if the one I just wrote sucks. Even if I don't think anybody's ever gonna wanna hear it. I don't know how not to write another one."

I absorb each word, recognizing the truth of them as my own. "Sometimes, I wish I knew how to unplug that need inside of me. How to reprogram myself to want to do something that wouldn't make my Mama so unhappy with my choices. That wouldn't force me to walk so far out on a ledge I'm terrified of falling off of."

He keeps his gaze on the street below us, and I have the feeling he's forcing himself not to look at me. I wonder if I've said too much, revealed enough vulnerability that I've made him uncomfortable.

But then he does look at me, his eyes locking onto mine, and I feel like he's drawing something up and out of me, a longing I've never felt before and am not even sure I could put a name to if asked. All I know is I can't make myself look away. Even though he just told me there's someone in his life. Even though every nerve ending is screaming at me to back up and go inside.

A car rolls by, its headlights throwing a shadow over us, and for a moment I see something in his face that I know as surely as I know my own name, I am in no way ready for. I sense that all I have to do to find out is place my hand on his chest, splay my fingers wide so that each tip absorbs the beat of his heart. In this moment, I want to do that as much as I have ever wanted to do anything. I close my eyes and imagine myself doing it or maybe I close them to stop myself from doing it.

"CeCe," he says.

My name is a protest, uttered to me or to himself, I don't know.

I let myself look at him then, and I feel the tug between us, as if an invisible cord now connects my heart to his. The stereo beat drums in my ears, and my pulse picks up its rhythm. I feel it in my wrists, my neck, the backs of my knees. My breathing has shortened, and I wilt forward like all the air has been let out of my bones.

His hands latch onto my shoulders, and he dips his head in, his mouth hovering over mine. I can smell the lemony scent of whatever soap he showered with. I tilt my head back, inviting him, imploring him.

When he steps away, I blink my eyes wide open and press a hand to my mouth.

"CeCe," he says, my name sounding ragged and torn. I haven't imagined that he wanted to kiss me. I can hear it in his voice, what it cost him to stop himself.

"What?" I manage, the question not really needing an answer.

"When the sun comes up, we'll wish we hadn't. You're gonna need a place to stay until you get things together. I'm okay with that. But this would just complicate everything."

He's right. I know it. "You always have this much common sense?" I ask.

"No," he says.

"Not sure I should be flattered by that."

"I can be stupid if you really want me to be." There's teasing in his voice, but something else, too. I could make him change his mind if I wanted to. I can hear that. Common sense is now raining down on me, and I take a step backwards.

"Think I'll try to get some sleep," I say.

His phone rings. He pulls it from his pocket, glances at the screen, then at me. "Goodnight then."

I step inside the apartment, close the door behind me, wondering if it's Sarah who's calling him in the middle of the night.

I start to walk toward the bedroom, then stop for a second, listening to the way his voice has changed. There's tenderness in it, longing, and I realize he must miss her.

I'm suddenly grateful for whatever bolt of logic kept us from following through on instinct just now. Holden might have moved to Nashville without Sarah, but he hasn't left her behind. Those are two very different things.

♪

Holden

Sarah's voice is soft and full of regret. I'm human, so it feels good to know that she wishes she'd come with us.

"I miss you so much," she says, and I can hear she's been crying.

"I miss you, too, baby." And I do. Way down deep to the core of me. Which in no way explains why I'd been out here wanting to kiss CeCe a few minutes ago, a girl I'd just met today.

"Everything feels empty without you. My bed, my apartment, the whole city of Atlanta feels empty without you."

Pride had kept her from saying any of this when I'd left early yesterday morning. Had it only been a day? Somehow, it feels like weeks since I had seen her.

"You know I want you here, too, Sarah. I never wanted to do this alone."

"And if I hadn't just gotten this promotion, I wouldn't have thought twice about it."

"I know." And I do. Sarah has a great job with an advertising firm in Atlanta. She's actually putting her college degree to use, and while, for her, singing with us was a side thing, something she did at night and on weekends, it's never been that for us.

For Thomas and me, music is THE thing, the ONLY thing we want to do.

Sometimes I think I could be happy living on an island eating bananas if all I had to do to survive was write and play.

Sarah grew up with a father who preached job security as the holy grail, the reason a person went to college in the first place, a means to increasing the likelihood that you would never be laid off, never wake up one morning to find that your livelihood had been snatched out from under you.

In all fairness, that's exactly what happened to him when Sarah was ten years old. They'd lost their house, their car, everything. Pretty much all they'd had left was the college fund he had put aside for Sarah.

I guess the thought of her squandering it by taking a shot on something less than for sure is more than he could stomach.

The sad thing is Sarah has a voice like an angel. I don't think she has any idea how good she really is. Maybe because it's not important to her in that way. Her voice is part of who she is, like the color of her hair, her height, or that she's a good runner. It doesn't define her.

As much as I love her, I know this is always going to be the fence between us.

"Did you play the Bluebird tonight?" she asks.

"Yeah," I say.

"How did it go?"

"It went great. Thomas sang the house down." I don't mention CeCe. It feels like I've left a big gaping hole in the truth of our day. Bringing up the fact that we picked up a girl on I-40 whose car caught on fire and then let her sing with us at the Bluebird when the person singing with us should have been Sarah, isn't a direction I want to take our conversation in.

"We had some interest from some record company guy," I say.

"Cool," she says, but I can hear the reserve in her voice. I really think what she wants to hear is that we don't have a shot in hell of making it so we'll come back to Atlanta with our tails tucked between our legs.

And suddenly, I'm feeling the same irritation I'd felt that morning when I left her in bed, warm from the quick urgent way in which we'd just made love. She'd begged me not to go, and I'd begged her to come with me.

The stalemate made us both angry and torn and frustrated.

"I've got to get up for a work in a bit," she says. "I should try to go back to sleep."

"You should," I say.

"Call me later?"

"Yeah. I will."

"Holden?"

"Yeah?"

"We'll work it out."

"We will."

"I miss you like crazy."

"I miss you, too."

She clicks off without saying goodbye. We made the agreement when we first met that we wouldn't use that word with each other. Sarah liked the idea that our time together never really ended if we didn't say goodbye. We just picked up where we left off.

I picture her in the bed we'd shared in her apartment, her long legs bare beneath the expensive sheets she'd insisted were worth splurging on. I wonder if she's staying on her side of the bed or if her arm is slung over my side, if she imagines I'm there with her as she tries to go to sleep.

I push off the deck railing and slip inside the apartment. I need to sleep. I walk down the hallway to the room where I can hear Thomas snoring. The door to CeCe's room is shut, but I stop outside it, touching my fingertips to the wood surface.

"Is someone there?" she calls out.

"It's just me," I say. "Sorry."

"That's all right," she answers.

I stand for a moment while neither of us says anything else. And then I go to my own room and close the door behind me.

♪

CeCe

The sun has found its way to every corner of the room when I wake up. Hank Junior is nowhere to be seen, and I scramble to my feet on a bolt of panic.

"Hanky?" I call out, opening the bedroom door and flying down the hall.

Thomas is standing in the small kitchen, pouring a bowl of cereal. "He's out walking with Holden."

The surprise of that brings me to a stop. "Oh. What time is it?"

"Ten."

"Ten?!? I can't believe I slept that long."

"Musta needed it." He offers me a red plastic cup and spoon. "Cereal?"

My stomach is growling loud enough for him to hear, so there's no use denying I'm hungry. "Thanks."

"I bought Hank Junior a couple cans of food while I was out. He's had his breakfast."

Gratitude washes over me in a wave. "How will I ever pay y'all back?"

"We're not lookin' for a payback."

"I didn't mean–"

"I know you didn't. Got us a newspaper, too," he says. "Job search central."

We take our cups and the paper and sit on the bare living room floor, spreading the sections out between us.

The door opens, and Holden and Hank Junior appear. Hank Junior trots over and gives me a slurpy kiss on the cheek, his tail wagging like he hasn't seen me in a year.

Holden is wearing running shorts. Hank Junior flops down beside me, panting big.

"We went for a jog," Holden says.

"Thanks for taking him," I say, and I cannot meet his gaze this morning.

43

He can't look at me either. The awkwardness between us is thick, nearly tangible in the room. I can't imagine what it would have felt like if we had continued what we started. I am overwhelmingly grateful that we didn't.

I feel Thomas looking at me, and then Holden before he says, "Did you two–" He stops, lasers Holden with a look. "Shiiiit, man. The only hound dog in this room is you."

"Quit talkin' crap, Thomas." Holden makes a show of pouring himself some cereal.

Thomas looks at me, raises an eyebrow. "Is it crap?"

"I don't know what you're talking about," I say.

"I must look like I just fell off the turnip truck," Thomas throws out.

"As a matter of fact," Holden says, joining us on the floor with his cereal.

Even though my cheeks feel hot, I put my focus on scanning through the Help Wanted section of the Classifieds, heartened by the number of places currently looking for waitstaff. "I have to get a job today," I say.

"We got you covered until you do," Thomas says.

"Thanks," I say. "Really. I don't know what I would have done without you."

"Good Samaritans R US," Thomas adds.

"What are you looking for?" Holden asks, not quite meeting my gaze.

"Waitressing."

"Go for the high end places," he says. "Big tips, and you never know who you'll meet."

"Are y'all looking for jobs?"

"Oh, yeah," Thomas says. "Waitin' tables ain't my thing. Got an interview over at the Mill and Feed. Throwin' bags of grain on a truck bed – that's me."

I smile and think he's right. I can't picture Thomas balancing a tray over a table full of picky people. "What about you, Holden?" I ask.

"Bartending," he answers. "That way I can write during the day. And if we get a gig, hopefully I can switch with someone else."

He pulls out his phone, taps an app and holds the screen up for me to see. "I've already made a list of the better places in town. If I'm going there, you might as well apply, too. To waitress, I mean."

"Oh, well, that would be–"

"I'll drive you both," Thomas says.

First thing I need to do is call Mama and ask for money. Thomas lets me borrow his phone again, and I slip into the bedroom and close the door. I know she won't recognize the number. I'm hoping she'll answer anyway.

She does, with a tentative hello.

"It's me, Mama," I say.

"CeCe. I've been calling your phone since last night. I was worried sick. Are you all right?"

"Yeah, I am. I had a little mishap."

"What happened?"

I picture her standing in our small kitchen, her hand worrying the long cord of the wall telephone. I know she's got a cigarette somewhere nearby because I can hear the smoke of it in her voice. I tell her the whole story then, hardly drawing in a breath until it's all out.

"Oh, CeCe," she says when I explain how I left the burned up car on the side of the Interstate for Triple A to have towed. "Where are you now?"

"I made a couple of friends. They're letting me crash at their place. They're really nice."

She doesn't ask, so I let her assume they are girls.

"Do you need me to come and get you?" she asks. "I can leave right–"

"No, Mama," I say, stopping her before the hope in her voice gets too much traction. "It's gonna be okay. I just wondered if you could wire me some cash. Until I get my credit card replaced and all that."

"Did you lose your purse, too?"

"Yeah."

"Oh, CeCe. Are you sure you're with nice people?"

"I am, Mama." And that really is one thing I can say for sure.

"Where should I send the money?"

I tap Thomas's Google app and do a local search for Western

Union. I give Mama the number. "I'll call you later today. I'm going job hunting. And I'll pay you back, okay?"

"I'm not worried about that, honey. You just be careful."

I know she's lonely. That she misses me. Guilt slips a noose around my neck, and I feel so selfish I can hardly stand myself. "Are you all right, Mama?"

"Why, sure I am," she says, her voice too bright, too cheery for me to believe her. "I've got choir practice tonight. We're having a coffee and dessert get together afterwards."

"That's good," I say. "What are you taking?"

We go on like this for a couple minutes until we both feel like some sort of normalcy has been reestablished between us, Mama not so worried, me not so guilty.

I miss her to the very deepest parts of me. In high school, I'd had so many friends who couldn't stand their mothers, who saw them as the one stumbling block between them and everything they wanted in life. I've never seen Mama as anything other than my biggest supporter and best friend. It's hard to leave that behind. Even to chase a dream.

Especially since I know how hard it was for her to let me go. She's never said it out loud, but I know she's terrified that I'll end up in the same place as my Uncle Dobie. That the love I have for music will be eclipsed by disillusion and defeat in the end, the two things that fueled his drinking. I've tried to reassure her many times. I've promised her I won't end up like that. But then she says that's what he said, too.

Tears well up in my eyes as I end the call. When I make it, the first thing I'll do is move Mama here and buy her a house that has everything she could ever want in it. She's so much a part of why I want to make it. I want to give her the things she's never been able to afford, provide her with a life that doesn't involve hoping there will be enough money in the checking account to pay off the month's bills.

I take a quick shower, without soap or shampoo. I stand in the tub until the water has dripped free of my skin, then squeeze out my hair, fluff it up with my fingers and pull it into a ponytail. At least I'm clean.

I feel fresh and rejuvenated. That seems like as good a place to start as any.

♪

THOMAS AND HOLDEN drive me to the Western Union, and I don't even have to wait to get my money. Mama must have left the house as soon as we hung up. Another wave of homesickness for her washes over me. Before we start hitting the restaurants for applications, I ask if we can make one more stop at a Goodwill store so I can buy some clothes.

Holden uses his local search to find one nearby, and Thomas drives there.

"You sure that's where you want to go?" he asks, looking at me with a raised eyebrow.

"You'd be surprised what you can find," I say.

They both go in with me, wandering the aisles and discussing their finds.

I'm after clothes, and I flip through the racks, not finding much at first. Then I spot a cute orange sundress in size 4 that looks like it will fit me. I grab it, along with a pair of black pants and a white shirt. A floral skirt and a light green t-shirt make up the rest of my stuff.

I head for the register and pay for my things. All of it comes to under $15.

Thomas and Holden are waiting in the truck. Thomas is flipping through an old book he'd found on how to make a guitar. Holden is writing something on one of the blank pages of his notebook.

He opens the door and slips out so I can slide in beside Hank Junior. "Find anything good?" he asks.

"I did," I say, feeling pleased with myself.

"I didn't know people actually shopped at Goodwill," Holden says.

I start to take this as an insult, except there's nothing judgmental in the assertion. It is simply that, a statement of fact.

"That's because you grew up with a silver spoon up your butt," Thomas throws out.

I expect Holden to snipe something back, but he just shakes his head. "At least I didn't grow up with cow manure between my toes."

"Neither one of them would make walking too easy," I say.

They both look at me then, and laugh, abruptly, as if I've surprised them. I rub Hank Junior's head and look down, a smile on my mouth.

Something warm unfurls within me, soft and fluttery as a butterfly. I like the feeling and realize it's something I haven't felt since high school, and even then, never like this.

Friendship.

♪

Holden

Based on my research, there are five restaurants in Nashville where I'd like to bartend. I came up with those by looking at potential nightly take, whether they're known for attracting the music business crowd, and their proximity to other clubs and bars in the city.

The first two are a total bust. The managers are tight-asses who start laying down the do's, the don'ts, and the musts like they're the last stop on Planet Great Job. I don't even let CeCe finish filling out the application. In both places, we leave them on the bar and head for the truck.

Thomas looks up from the nap he'd been trying to take and gives me a look I've seen before. "I assume they didn't pass your personality test?"

"Whatever hours I have to give away to support this gig, I'm not giving to either of them."

"They seemed nice enough," CeCe says, and I can tell she thinks I might be a little nuts.

We're on 40, heading for downtown when I look at her and say, "How many jobs have you had?"

She's quiet for a few moments. "If you count the three day stint at McDonald's, two."

My eyes go wide. I can't help it. "Where was the other one?"

"Beckner's Veterinary Clinic."

I consider this and then say, "Seriously? So you have no actual waitressing experience?"

"No," she admits. "But I've watched a lot of them during shows."

"How are you planning to write that up on the app? Conducted observations of working waitresses in real-life settings? Or served breakfast, lunch, and dinner to canine and feline guests at Chez Beckner?"

Thomas lets loose a bark of a laugh, as if it surprises him. He apologizes for it, looking at CeCe and saying, "Sorry. He's an ass. But a sometimes funny ass."

CeCe doesn't seem to think so. "I'll be a great waitress," she says, folding her arms across her chest.

"Places like these usually don't want to just take your word for it."

Thomas wheels the truck into the third place on my list, backing into a shady spot at one end of the parking lot. "Can you two finish your argument on the way in so I can catch some shut-eye, please?"

I get out, pissed enough at CeCe that I start across the pavement without waiting up for her until I get to the front door.

"I don't have to apply at the same places as you," she says, stopping in front of me, an expression of stubborn pride on her face.

"I don't care if you apply here or anywhere else," I say. "I was just pointing out that you usually need some experience for places like this."

"I get that."

"Okay then," I say while we glare at each other.

I look away first, start to open the restaurant door, and then on impulse, turn back to her. "About last night–"

"Wasn't that a movie?" she quips.

"Look," I begin again awkwardly.

She holds up a hand to stop me. "You really don't need to go there. You have a girlfriend. Moment of weakness. No explanation needed."

Her straightforwardness surprises me. "Yeah. Something like that."

"So we're past it," she says. "Moving on?"

I'm not sure what I was expecting. It wasn't this. The girls I've known are way more persistent. Or maybe it's just my ego that's feeling the air leak.

I open the door and leave her to walk in behind me, just on principle.

The restaurant's foyer is low lit, and I blink a couple of times to adjust to the dimness. The dining room is big and circular, the walls a deep red, the tablecloths on each of the tables a rich gold. The bar is at the back. It's enormous, carved walnut, I think, and it looks like the kind of place where major movers and shakers would want to hang out.

"Wow," CeCe says in a low, breathy voice.

"Yeah. Wow," I agree. There's no one in sight, and so I call out a, "Hello?"

When there's no answer, CeCe says, "It doesn't look like anyone is here."

Still ticked at her, I ignore her and walk toward the bar. I call hello again, but still no one comes.

I look around the corner of the bar. There's a long hallway that looks like it has two or three offices on either side.

"Maybe we should come back," CeCe says behind me, sounding worried.

I'm anxious to get a job nailed down, and this looks like the place I was hoping for. I head down the hall, raising my voice again, "Hello?"

I hear something and stick my head inside the next office doorway. CeCe bumps into me, jostling me forward just as I realize what I am staring at.

A man on top of a woman on top of a desk, naked as Adam and Eve before the apple thing.

I catch myself just before my forehead hits the opposite end of the doorjamb, CeCe grabbing my shirt to keep from falling.

"Oh, my gosh!" she says, spotting what I've just spotted.

Both the man and the woman look at us then, and amazingly enough, neither of them jumps up in alarm or embarrassment or anything resembling either one.

My gaze snags first on her, fortyish, blonde, gorgeous, and then on the man, whose face is instantly recognizable. Case Phillips. Case-frigging-Phillips!

I jerk upright and turn my back to face the hallway. CeCe does the same, and I guess we must look like two soldiers snapping to attention after a reprimand.

"I'm sorry," I say. "We were looking for the manager or–"

"Owner?" the woman asks.

"Owner," I agree, still not looking.

"That would be me. And I'm a little–"

"Occupied. You're occupied. We can come back."

She laughs. "Why don't you do that?"

"Ah, are you looking for any bartending help?"

A couple beats of silence pass. "I think I just might be."

"Good. How about waitressing? Need any?"

"That depends on the waitress."

"That would be me," CeCe pipes up, raising a hand and waving it in the air. She starts to glance over her shoulder, but I throw my arm around her and tuck her into my side, so she can't.

"Why don't you two come see me later this afternoon when I'm not–"

"Indisposed," the man on top of her says with a chuckle. And in the notes of his laugh, I hear the voice I've heard on the radio a thousand times. Again, shit!

"Indisposed," the woman agrees, laughing.

I hear feet hit the floor, just before the door behind us slams shut. And then Case Phillips: "Shoulda shut the damn thing to start with."

"Come here and let me make it up to you," she says.

Only then do I let myself look down at CeCe. She's pressing her lips together, like laughter is about to explode out of her. I grab her arm and haul her down the hallway before she wrecks whatever opportunity we might have.

By the time we reach the dining room, we're both running full out, through the foyer, the front door, all the way to Thomas's truck before we collapse against the passenger side door and can't hold it back a second longer.

We laugh until my eyes are watering, and we've woken up Thomas. He slides out and walks around to look down at us like we're both insane.

"What the heck?" he asks.

I start to tell him, but I still can't talk.

"We just saw Case Phillips naked as a jaybird in there on top of the woman who owns this place." She tries to stop, then starts up laughing again.

"Was she naked, too?" Thomas asks, straight-faced.

"Oh, yeah," I say.

"Well, all right then," Thomas says.

CeCe is giggling so hard now she can barely breathe.

I glance across the parking lot and spot the black Ferrari tucked into a corner space. The license plate says JSTNCASE.

I point at it, and Thomas lets out a low whistle. "That's the life I want. The car and the girl."

"I hope I'm not the one that finds your bare linebacker ass on top of some hot babe," I say, wiping my eyes.

CeCe giggles a fresh giggle. "Don't need that visual."

Thomas laughs. "Don't knock it till you've tried it."

I get to my feet then, offering CeCe a hand up. She stands and for a second tips into my chest, her breasts soft and full against me. I feel the shock as if someone just stuck a hot wire to my back. Our gazes lock for a snap of a second, and I see the same awareness in her eyes.

I step away, too quickly, and hang my running shoe on Thomas's enormous cowboy boot. I catch myself before hitting the pavement, and grab onto the bed of the truck.

"Good day, man," Thomas says, "you are in such a world of trouble."

"Shut up, Thomas," I say, climbing in. "All I pay you to do is drive."

Chuckling, Thomas shakes his head and pulls CeCe around to his side, waiting while she slides into the middle of the seat.

I lower my window, keeping as close to the door as I can.

♪

CeCe

So it's decided once we get to the apartment that I will buy in as a roommate. Both Thomas and Holden say they don't mind rooming together.

"I already know how bad his boots can stink," Holden had graciously said.

"And I already know what kind of rattlesnake he is at six a.m.," Thomas throws back, matching the dig.

What it adds up to is the two of them throwing me a lifeline. Since I am now starting out in Nashville from negative ground zero thanks to the explosion of Granny's car, I don't have any choice but to take it.

And I am grateful. I tell them both as much, promising to pay them every penny I owe them.

"Ah, don't worry about it," Thomas says once we're at the apartment, and I am again scouring the classifieds, Hank Junior asleep with his head on my lap. Holden had borrowed Thomas's truck to go open up a banking account. I'm not holding out hope for the Case Phillips joint, considering that I've now seen the owner naked. Seems like a significant conflict of interest to me.

"I will worry about it," I say. "I like to pay my debts."

"In other words, you don't like letting others do something for you."

"Only a fool rejects a helping hand when it's needed, but I believe in keeping the slate clean, too."

"You and pecker head are more alike than you know."

I glance up from the paper, raise an eyebrow.

"Holden," he says, like who else would he be talking about.

I refuse to acknowledge the comparison, and say, "They've got openings at the Olive Garden."

"Love the food, but how's that going to help your music?"

"By helping me pay my way around here, feed myself and Hank Junior."

"Holden's right about putting yourself in a place where music stuff is happening."

"In Nashville, that could be at McDonald's."

"True. But the odds are greater over there where Case Phillips is getting some."

"Girl here. You and Holden are going to have to remember this isn't a locker room."

Thomas grins. "Spunk. I like it."

Just then the apartment door swings open, and Holden bursts through, his big white smile the first thing I see.

"You're not going to believe who I just saw in Whole Foods!"

Thomas and I both stare at him, waiting.

"Taylor Swift."

"Seriously?" Thomas throws out.

"Picking out apples in the produce department."

"You suck," Thomas says. "Did you ask for her autograph?"

Holden tosses him a look. "Right after I taped that sign to my forehead that says 'New to Nashville and gawking at every star'."

"Well, you've seen two already today. You might want to let someone else borrow your sign," Thomas argues, sounding irked.

I laugh. I can't help it. The two of them are pretty ridiculous. "Y'all are like two old ladies at a bachelor auction," I say.

"I've got a lyric I want to work on," Holden says, ignoring me and grabbing a Coke from the refrigerator before heading for the back of the apartment.

"To give you a heads up on the vernacular," Thomas says, looking at me, "that means don't come anywhere near him until he comes out and gives the okay."

"Ah," I say.

"If you do bother him, I recommend a shield of some sort. A baking sheet works pretty well."

"Because?"

"He's gonna throw something at you."

I laugh again. "How in the world did the two of you ever get hooked up?"

"Football was the original connect. He had a daddy to prove wrong. And I had a mama to prove right."

"How so?"

Thomas digs his spoon into the half-gallon of chocolate ice cream in front of him. "Holden's father didn't think he had what it took to play ball."

"Why?"

Thomas shrugs. "The real answer is he's pretty much a jerk. He kind of thinks being a musician waters down any athleticism gene."

"Why would he think that?"

"Heck if I know. Why does anyone think stupid stuff?"

I find myself feeling a pang of empathy for Holden. My mama and I never had much, but if I said I wanted to fly to the moon, she'd start helping me make the wings. "What did you have to prove to your mom?" I ask.

"That I was as good as she thought I was."

"That's nice."

"Better than Holden's version for sure."

"How long has he been writing?"

"Since kindergarten."

"I mean lyrics."

"Since kindergarten."

We both smile, and I say, "He's the real thing, huh?"

"As it gets."

"He's lucky to have you to write for."

"Actually, I'm the lucky one. I can sing until the cows come home, but hand me a pencil and tell me to write something that's gonna strike a chord with somebody, and my brain freezes up like lemonade in Alaska."

"You're lucky to have each other then."

"I'll go with that." He looks at me a moment, and then, "What's your dream, CeCe? Why are you in Nashville?"

"To sing and write."

"If you had to pick one, what would it be?"

"I love both, but unlike Holden, other than myself I don't have anyone else to write for, so if I had to pick one, I guess it would be singing."

"You're good, you know. Real good."

I hear the sincerity in his voice, and I start to brush off the compliment like it's no big deal. Actually, it is. I bask in it for a second or two. "Thank you for that. I appreciate it."

"I guess you know there are hundreds of others here just like us. Fresh off the bus. Totally sold on their talent. Ready to share it with the world."

"Yeah," I say, the seriousness in his voice instantly sobering me up from the high of his praise.

"So you wanna know what the difference between me and them is?"

Again, "Yeah."

"I've got the work ethic of a dozen mules. If someone offers me a gig down on the corner of Broadway at two in the afternoon, I'm gonna take it 'cause you never know who might be walking by. Every single chance I get to open my mouth and sing, that's what I'm gonna be doing. And I ain't averse to shakin' some hands and kissin' some babies either."

Laughter bursts up out of me, part delight, part amazement. "You're going the politician route then?"

"It don't matter what talent you've got if people don't like you first. If you're an ass, they won't bother looking past that long enough to see any other good in you."

"Aren't you a little young to be this wise?"

"My granddaddy was in Georgia politics. By the time I was six years old, I'd watched him win voter after voter just by being nice to them. It wasn't an act on his part. He genuinely liked people. Enjoyed hearing what they had to say. He taught me that you end up with way more in this world if you go at it by giving back first."

"You're amazing," I say and mean it.

He looks surprised by that and practically blushes. "Naw."

"You are."

"Holden's right about my boots," he says, grinning.

I laugh. "Even so."

He gets up to throw away his ice cream carton and put his spoon in the sink. I want to thank him, but the words stick in my throat, and I can't force them out. "Thomas?" I say, my voice cracking.

"Yeah," he calls back over his shoulder.

"I'm really glad y'all stopped yesterday. I don't know how I got that lucky."

He turns around then, studies me as if he knows just what I'm trying to say. And when he says, "No, CeCe, I think Holden and I are gonna turn out to be the lucky ones," I know for sure Thomas would make his granddaddy proud.

♪

Holden

CeCe hasn't said a word since we left the apartment. I'm matching her silence beat for beat, determined not to speak first.

"Don't you think this is a waste of time?" she finally asks just as we turn in at the restaurant parking lot.

"Actually, no, I don't," I say, swinging into a spot at the back. I glance at the corner of the building where the Ferrari had been parked earlier. "Looks like Case is gone anyway."

"Oh, good," CeCe says. "I've seen enough naked country music stars for one day."

"You sure about that?"

"Quite."

"I mean we could ask her when he's coming back," I say, enjoying myself.

"No, thank you."

We both get out of the truck, slam our respective doors and walk side by side into the main entrance of the restaurant. Unlike earlier, now all the lights are on, and wait staff bustle around table to table getting the place ready for evening business.

A man in a dark suit and a blazing red tie walks up and says, "Can I help you?"

"We're here to see Ms. Trace," I say.

"Is she expecting you?"

I nod yes, hoping like heck she remembers.

"Just a moment." He walks through and disappears down the hallway behind the bar.

CeCe and I stand poker still in the foyer, and if I feel like a fish out of water, it's clear that she does, too.

Ten minutes later, the blonde woman we'd met in her birthday suit just a few hours before walks in wearing a sexy-as-all-get-out black dress that leaves little to the imagination as to why Case Phillips hangs here.

"You came back," she says, looking directly at me.

I sense, rather than hear, CeCe stepping up close behind me. I move aside so Ms. Trace can see her too. "Yeah," I say. "We were hoping you'd have a moment to talk to us."

"Sure." She waves us both to the bar, pulls a chair up and sits down. "Have a seat."

Remembering my manners, I pull out one for CeCe, causing the woman to raise an eyebrow in approval. I take the next chair over.

"So you're looking to bartend," she says, her assessing blue gaze on me.

"Yes, ma'am," I say.

"And I was hoping you might have a waitressing position open," CeCe throws in.

"What kind of experience do you both have?"

"I tended bar around the University of Georgia," I say.

"You go there?"

"I did."

"Played ball, I bet."

"Yeah."

"You any good?"

"They seemed to think I was."

"But music's your real love," she says.

"Yeah," I admit, wondering how many guys just like me had sat here asking her for a job. Based on her look, I'm assuming a lot.

"How about you?" she asks, glancing at CeCe.

I hold my breath, hoping she's not going to tell her about the veterinary clinic.

"I've never actually waitressed," CeCe says, while I cringe inside. "But I am a really hard worker. I've watched some great waitresses in places where I've had gigs. I'd like to think I've filed away what works and what doesn't."

To my surprise, Ms. Trace looks impressed.

"Hm. Most girls would have told me they had experience even when they didn't."

"The truth is a lot less cumbersome," CeCe says.

"You're right about that. It just so happens I do have a couple of open spots. The bartending position is about thirty hours a week, the waitressing one more like fifteen. You okay to start with that?"

"Yeah," we both say in unison.

"Can you start tonight?"

"Yeah," we echo again.

Ms. Trace smiles. "Uniforms are in the back. The ones hanging in plastic have been dry-cleaned. See if you can find something in your size, and we'll get started."

She stands and leads the way, showing us where the uniforms are.

"All right, then. I'll tell Michael, the manager up front to show you two the ropes."

"Thank you, Ms. Trace."

"Yes, thank you," CeCe adds.

She looks at me then, her gaze direct and unless I'm mistaken, slightly interested.

"It's Lauren," she says.

"Thank you. Lauren," I say.

"You're welcome. Both of you." And with that, she turns and heads to the main part of the restaurant.

"Wowww," CeCe says once she's out of earshot.

"What?"

"That look."

"What look?

"You know what look."

"No, I don't."

"Yes, you do."

"What are we? Six?"

CeCe smiles. "She doesn't think you're six."

I roll my eyes and start looking at pants hanging in the closet. I find a pair of thirty-twos, pull out those and a white long sleeve shirt in large.

CeCe steps up and rifles through the skirts in her size. I notice that she finds a four and a white blouse in a small.

"I'm not changing in here with you," she says.

I roll my eyes again. "Like I want you to."

I leave in search of the men's room, figuring she can find the women's on her own. Once I've changed, I head for the bar. Michael, the guy in the black suit, is waiting there. He starts showing me the setup behind and spends the next ten minutes or so telling me who some of their customers are, what they like, the drinks the restaurant likes to push. Some of the names he drops are pretty impressive, I have to admit.

"Here's what's not cool," he says. "I'm assuming you're here for the music business, and this is a secondary gig to you."

I don't bother denying it.

"When these folks come in, they want to be away from all that. Not ever cool to pitch a song, ask for a card, give a card, a lyric, a CD."

I laugh. "I take it that's been done before?"

"Ohh, yeah."

"Got it. Not cool."

He turns to CeCe then where she's been waiting at the end of the bar for him to finish with me. "Why don't we start there? Did you get that part?"

"Yeeaah. I got that part. Does that include live auditions while I'm serving dessert?"

Now he laughs. "Yeah. It includes that."

CeCe smiles. "Not cool."

He looks at me. "You good?"

I nod. "Yep."

CeCe follows him to the front of the restaurant where he begins introducing her to some of the other wait staff. I watch her shake hands with them, notice how easily her smile comes when it's not being censored for me. A blonde dude with a GQ face holds her hand longer than necessary. It's clear that CeCe isn't immune to its intensity, and it feels kind of weird seeing her melt a bit under it.

I start taking glasses from the dishwasher and placing them on the shelf behind the bar. So she thinks the guy is hot. Whatever.

♪

CeCe

I think I'm gonna like waitressing. By nine o'clock, I have two hundred dollars in my tip wallet. I haven't spilled a thing. And not one person has yelled at me. I'm beginning to see why Holden insisted on making this place first choice. Two hundred dollars in three hours. Not bad.

And that's not even counting the fact that Brad Paisley and his wife Kimberly are having dinner in one of the private rooms off the main area. Not part of my station, but cool nonetheless.

From the looks of it, Holden has been knocking back some good money as well, the bar slammed non-stop. I haven't really recognized anyone, except Brad Paisley, of course. Everyone here appears uber-successful at something or other. Hair and makeup are flawless. Suits are definitely high end. And the women's shoes alone, purchase price all total, could make a ding in the national debt.

Thomas comes in around eight to get the truck keys from Holden. He's been downtown going bar to bar, trying to book some gigs. He took the bus over. The plan is for him to pick Holden and me up when we get off after eleven.

Thomas agrees to head back to the apartment and take Hank Junior out for a walk since I am sure he's about to pee in his fur.

When the last of the customers leave the restaurant, I feel as if my feet have permanently molded themselves to the insides of my shoes. Cleanup takes an hour or better, and it's after midnight before we're done. Holden finishes before I do, and he's waiting by the front door when I say goodnight to the other waiters and waitresses and head out.

In the parking lot, Holden says, "I decided not to call Thomas since it's so late. Okay with you to take the bus?"

"Sure," I say, and we walk to the curb, sitting down on the bench to wait. We're the only ones at the stop, and there's very little traffic on the street in front of us.

"So how was it?" he asks, leaning back to stare up at the sky, his arms folded across his chest.

"Actually, pretty amazing."

"You like?"

"I like."

"You're welcome."

"Thank you."

"Don't mention it."

I smile. "Did you know Brad Paisley came in?"

"I took a bottle of champagne to his table. Dom on the house."

I bolt around to face him. "No fair!"

"Fair."

"What did he say?!?"

"Thank you very much."

"Is that it?"

"That's it."

"Were you nervous?"

He raises his head to look at me. "He's a person like the rest of us."

"A person, yes. Like the rest of us, no."

"How you figure?"

"Just blazingly talented, that's all."

"Agreed. Got a pretty wife, too."

"I'm sure you noticed."

"Do I look dead?"

"Only a bit."

"Thanks," he says with a surprised grin.

"You're welcome."

"How'd you do tonight?"

"Crazy good. Three hundred and some change by the end of the night."

"Awesome."

"How 'bout you?"

"A little better than that."

"People must be generous when they're drinking."

"Alcohol is a well-known lubricant for the wallet."

The bus rolls up and screeches to a stop. Holden stands and waits for me to step through the open door. We find a seat in the back, and we're a few minutes into the ride when I make myself say, "Thanks for helping me get the job, Holden. I know I wouldn't have if you hadn't been there."

"Oh, I don't know. I think she liked your honesty."

"She liked your body."

He tilts his head to look at me with a raised eyebrow. "Yeah?"

"Yeah," I say, something warm unfurling in my chest.

"Do you like it?" he asks, his voice warm and curious.

"I think your head has been enlarged quite enough for one day."

He laughs. "It's awfully easy to yank your chain."

"Is not."

"Is, too."

I huff a big sigh and turn my head to look out the window, but I'm smiling. Holden seems to have that effect on me.

♪

Holden

We get to the apartment to find that Thomas isn't there. The truck is parked out front, but he's nowhere to be found. And neither is Hank Junior.

"Could he have taken him for another walk?" CeCe asks.

"Probably. I'll text him and see."

"Okay," she says, fixing herself a glass of ice water.

I tap the message into my phone.

Me: Hey. Where r u

Thomas: Looking 4 hank jr

Me: What do u mean looking

Thomas: As in I can't find him

Me: Wtf

Thomas: A squirrel ran out when I was walking him and he took off

Me: Seriously?

Thomas: So

Me: We took the bus. Where r u and we'll help look

Thomas: R u gonna break the news to CeCe

Me: Yeah. Thanks 4 that.

Thomas: Shit

Me: So

She's left the kitchen, and I walk down the hall to her room. Feeling like I just swallowed a rock, I stick my head inside the open door. "Ah, CeCe?"

She comes out of the bathroom, toothbrush in her hand. "Yeah?"

"Thomas kind of lost Hank Junior."

"What do you mean lost?" she asks slowly.

"He took off after a squirrel, and Thomas dropped the leash."

Her face loses its color. "How long ago?"

"I'm not sure."

"Where is Thomas?"

"Still looking."

She grabs a pair of running shoes off the floor and tugs them on. "Can you find out where he's been so I can try a different area?"

I call Thomas this time, instead of texting. He picks up on the first ring and tells me which streets he's covered. "Why don't y'all start with the ones closest to the apartment?" he says. "In case he headed back that way?"

"Okay. Call you in a few."

We click off, and I glance at CeCe who now looks as if she might be physically sick. "Come on," I say, squelching my pity and forcing myself to focus on finding the dog. "Don't worry. He's probably not far away."

We head down Fume Street. CeCe's voice is high and sweet in the way she sounds calling for Hank Junior to come when it's time to eat. We walk to the end of Fume, then cut across to Sharp and jog all the way down. I wonder how many people we're waking up, then realize immediately that I don't care as long as we find Hank Junior.

Aside from calling him, CeCe hasn't said a word. I see in the rigid set of her shoulders and the tenseness of her jaw that she's barely holding it together.

We've just started up another street when a porch light flips on at a house we're about to pass. A woman comes out in a fluffy white robe and waves a hand at us. We both stop, and she bustles over, a worried look on her face. "Are you looking for a dog?"

"Yes," CeCe says quickly. "A Walker Hound. White with black and tan markings."

"Oh, yes." She shakes her head. "Animal control picked him up a little over an hour ago. I heard some barking and came outside. My neighbor, that crotchety old Mr. Lemmons, name fitting, I might add, had already called the pound because the dog had been in his yard for a half hour or more."

"But he had ID on his collar," CeCe says, her voice breaking on the end.

"I could see that, and I told the officer that we could call the number on the tag. He said he didn't have time to wait."

"The phone number on that tag is my cell, and I don't have it now." CeCe looks at me with eyes brimmed over with tears.

"Did you happen to see a name on the truck?" I ask the woman. "So we'll know where to go to get him?"

"Davidson County Animal Control," she says. "I asked him where he would be taking him, and he said the main facility."

"Thank you," I say to the woman, just as CeCe turns and takes off running down the street. We all but sprint the entire way to the apartment, and I have to admit I'm impressed with her stamina.

I call Thomas as soon as we're back in the parking lot of our place and tell him what we know.

"Take the truck," he says. "I'm still a few blocks away."

"Okay. I'll let you know what we find out."

"Tell her I'm sorry, okay?"

"She knows."

I end the call and wave CeCe to the truck. "Let's go. Thomas said to take it and that he's sorry."

CeCe nods, and doesn't speak because she's about to burst out crying again. I Google the animal control place and then tap the address into my GPS. It's a good haul from us, and we don't say a word the entire drive. She just sits straight up in the seat, staring ahead as if she's willing the distance between her and her dog to melt into nothingness.

The building is off the main road, and an intimidating gate blocks the entrance. The truck's headlights illuminate the sign. NO TRESPASSING. HOURS OF OPERATION 8 AM – 4 PM

A chain link fence surrounds the property, and a camera sits on one corner of the gate. "This place is locked up like Fort Knox," I say.

"There has to be some way we can get in," CeCe says, tears in her voice. She slides out of the truck and jogs over, jerking at the padlock.

I walk up behind her, put my hand on her shoulder. "We can wait here until they open."

She looks up at me, her eyes wide and hurt-filled. "But he's in there."

"I know."

"What if they–"

"He'll be okay until morning," I say, hoping like heck that I'm right.

"We could climb the fence."

"And then what? We won't be able to get in the building."

"Someone might be there."

"I doubt it since the gate is closed."

"I want to make sure." She grabs the chain link and starts to climb.

I grab her around the waist and haul her off, swinging her away from it. She slides to the ground in front of me, and I'm instantly aware of her breasts against my chest, her thighs pressing into mine. With one arm around her, I carry her to the truck. I open the driver's side door and set her on the seat, facing me. "He's gonna be okay," I say.

She starts to cry outright then, and I realize she's been doing her best to hold it in since finding out Hank Junior was missing. Hearing her cry feels like someone just stuck a knife in my heart, and I push a hand through her hair and pull her up against me. Her cheek is against my chest, and I draw her closer, wanting to absorb her pain.

I rub her back with one hand, my other anchored in her long, sweet-smelling hair. She widens the space between her knees, and I step in closer, some kind of crazy need sweeping up through me.

She raises her face to mine, and I can't stop myself from kissing her. It's not the right time. And it's not for the right reasons. I know this, but I can't stop.

I can feel how much she wants to escape from where we are, blank out what has happened tonight. I guess I do, too, or at least that's what I tell myself. It's a lot easier to know what to do with that than it is knowing what to do with the fact that I'm kissing her because there's nothing in the world I want to do more right now than exactly that.

♪

CeCe

Nothing in my life has ever felt as good as Holden's kiss. Not the top of my first roller coaster ride, right before the plunge. Or the first time I performed one of my own songs in front of a crowd. Not even the day my Uncle Dobie said he thought I had a future in country music.

At first, Holden is gentle, kissing me like he's not sure where the line is. I'm the one who deepens it. I loop my arms around his neck and pull him closer, opening my mouth beneath his and inviting him in. He accepts. I've never been kissed like this. Thoroughly. Completely. Expertly.

And that's what it feels like. As if Holden knows exactly how to coax, persuade, entice. A couple minutes of this, and my mind is blanked of everything but him. I explore the ripples of abs. His breathing quickens, and I trace the other side.

He runs his hands down my back and under my bottom to anchor me up against him, as if he needs me to know what I'm doing to him. Knowing I'm not ready for what I've so clearly asked him for, I pull away and study his far too good-looking face, my chest feeling as if I've just run a marathon.

"I'm sorry, Holden," I say.

He smooths my hair back from my face. "If this ever happens between us, it has to be for the right reasons."

Sanity begins to wash over me in a wave. And along with it, a tide of mortification. "Thank you."

He laughs. "Thank you?"

"For taking my mind off Hank Junior for a few minutes."

"It was entirely my pleasure. Should I feel used?"

"Maybe a little."

"It's not so bad, being used by you."

I smile, then just as quickly feel the tears well back up and spill down my cheeks.

Holden physically slides me to the middle of the seat and climbs in, shutting the door. He hooks an arm around me and tucks me into the curve of his shoulder. "He's going to be all right," he says. "We can wait here until someone comes to open up."

"You don't have to stay with me."

"I want to."

"Why?" I ask, my voice muffled against his shirt.

Holden glances out the window. "We had a dog when I was growing up. A yellow Lab named Lucy."

He's silent for a bit, and I say, "Yeah?"

"Our yard was fenced, but some of the kids in the neighborhood unlatched the gate one day when we weren't home. She got out, and that night after we came back, we looked everywhere. The next morning, my mom called the pound to make sure she wasn't there, and they said she wasn't. We put up flyers and kept looking for days. Every day my mom called and gave them her description again. They kept telling her she wasn't there."

My stomach drops, and I'm not sure I want to hear the rest of this. But I wait, unable to tell him that.

"Someone my dad knew called and said he'd just heard we were missing our dog. He had seen a yellow Lab at the pound when he and his family went down to adopt a puppy."

I want to say something. I can't because it feels like my voice is locked up inside me.

"My mom and dad and I jumped in the car and drove to the pound as fast as we could. Mom showed a woman at the front desk Lucy's picture, and just the look on her face made me run out of the place."

"Oh, Holden."

"We'd been calling for days, and they said she wasn't there."

I hear the bitterness behind the words, and I can barely bring myself to ask, "Did they–"

"The woman said they'd held her for the required period of time, but when the kennels became full–"

I reach up and touch my fingers to his lips. Tears run down my face, and I'm not surprised to see that the same is true for Holden. I lean in and kiss each of them away, my heart feeling as if it has splintered into a thousand pieces.

We sit silent for what feels like a long time, me absorbing, Holden reliving, I guess.

And then he finally says, "When I think about someone leading her to some room and taking her life while she's wondering where we are. . .while we're looking for her–"

A sob rises up out of me, this image of Lucy more than I can manage right now. Sorrow for her and renewed fear for Hank Junior swallow me.

Holden pulls me closer, and while I know I should be comforting him, he's the one comforting me. "So that's why I want to wait here with you," he says.

I've barely known Holden for any time at all. It feels like I've known him forever.

♪

WE'RE QUIET FOR the next hour or so, arms locked around one another, like we both need this mutual infusion of empathy and understanding.

The truck's digital clock says 4:07 when Holden reaches beneath the seat and pulls out a notebook. I sit up and watch him remove a pencil from the spiral binding.

"What is it?" I ask.

"Just a thought for a lyric."

He writes a line on the blank page.

> So I got a few things I need to say

He's still for a bit before writing:

> Never thought my life would turn out this way

His pencil is quiet again. This time several minutes pass before he writes down:

> Do you ever think about the choice you made
> And what those who loved her have had to pay

Then he adds:

> Chorus
> What you took from me
> You can't give back

I wait for the next line, trying to guess what it might be. Several minutes pass before he writes:

                    You took the sun
                    You took the stars
              You took the ground beneath my feet
     The words are out before I realize I've said them. "You even took
the air I breathe."
     Holden looks at me and nods. He writes it down.
                    You even took the air I breathe
And then adds:
              Everything, that's what you took from me
     "For Lucy," I say.
     "I don't know what else it will end up being. I never do at this
point."
     The sun has started to lighten the horizon behind the pound
building. I feel a settling sense of peace that it's all gonna be okay. That
very soon, I'll have Hank Junior back, that his fate will be different
from Lucy's. Holden's sweet Lucy.
     Sitting here with him as he writes on his rumpled pad, I have no
way of knowing that in a few months, one of Nashville's most well-
known artists will hear Thomas singing Holden's song, the one he
started in this truck with me, at a club downtown. Or that in a year and
a half, that same artist, whose wife was killed by a drunk driver, will
release it, and the song will hit number one.
     Looking at him now, the intensity on his good-looking face, my
heart feels like it's becoming aware for the very first time of what it was
made to feel. It's both terrifying and wonderful all at once.
     He has a girlfriend. I know this, but my heart isn't listening. Just
like it hasn't listened to all the reasons why turning my dreams over to
Nashville might not have been the safest route for me to take.
     Some things, our hearts don't let us have a say in. For me, music is
one. And right here, right now, I believe Holden Ashford might be the
other.
     Someone once said every new beginning comes from some other
beginning's end. The trick then has to be letting go of the safe, the
known and reaching out for what we can't yet see.
     I'm ready to reach.
     I really am.

♪

More of CeCe, Holden, Thomas and Hank Junior

Made in the USA
Monee, IL
04 September 2020